BOLAN'S MESSAGE

"Who's your boss?"

"Uh—God, I dunno. Wait! Now wait! Give me time to lay it out! I—"

"Kiss your ass goodbye, Jingo," Bolan icily advised him.

"Hey, we never see the guy. God's truth. He's not one of us—that's all I know."

"Okay, okay," Morelli sighed. "He's got a code name. They call him Trooper. Now that's the all of it, I swear. I never seen the guy. I don't know nobody that did. The contact is always by telephone or radio. He's got a secret base up here, somewhere. He runs everything from there."

"Tell him I've come for him, Jingo. Tell him I got his message. Tell him."

Bolan's numbers had run out. Already too much time had been spent here, at the edge of the death zone.

The Executioner Series:

#1 WAR AGAINST THE MAFIA
#2 DEATH SQUAD
#3 BATTLE MASK
#4 MIAMI MASSACRE
#5 CONTINENTAL CONTRACT
#6 ASSAULT ON SOHO
#7 NIGHTMARE IN NEW YORK
#8 CHICAGO WIPEOUT
#9 VEGAS VENDETTA
#10 CARIBBEAN KILL
#11 CALIFORNIA HIT
#12 BOSTON BLITZ
#13 WASHINGTON I.O.U.
#14 SAN DIEGO SIEGE
#15 PANIC IN PHILLY
#16 SICILIAN SLAUGHTER
#17 JERSEY GUNS
#18 TEXAS STORM
#19 DETROIT DEATHWATCH
#20 NEW ORLEANS KNOCKOUT
#21 FIREBASE SEATTLE
#22 HAWAIIAN HELLGROUND
#23 ST. LOUIS SHOWDOWN
#24 CANADIAN CRISIS
#25 COLORADO KILL-ZONE

PINNACLE BOOKS • NEW YORK CITY

This is a work of fiction. All the characters and events portrayed in this book are fictional, and any resemblance to real people or incidents is purely coincidental.

THE EXECUTIONER: COLORADO KILL-ZONE

An original Pinnacle Books edition, published for the first time anywhere.

ISBN: 0-523-00824-4

First printing, March 1976

Cover illustration by Gil Cohen

Printed in Canada

PINNACLE BOOKS, INC.
275 Madison Avenue
New York, N.Y. 10016

We fight rather to keep something
alive than in the expectation that
anything will triumph.
—T. S. Eliot

Win, hell! Nobody wins this game.
Survival, that's all. But it's enough.
—Mack Bolan, the Executioner

Dedicated to all the good friends in Colorado—especially to the Martin Men—and the pleasant memories thereof.

dp

TABLE OF CONTENTS

Colorado Kill-Zone

PROLOGUE

War machine—one-man army—kill specialist—*Executioner*: these were some of the appellations adhering to Mack Bolan through two combat tours in Southeast Asia. It was an extraordinary time, and it developed extraordinary men, most of whom came home when their time was over and found for themselves a variety of ordinary niches in a sometimes less than ordinary existence.

There was nothing ordinary about Mack Bolan's homecoming. He returned not to the warmth and comfort of the family home in Pittsfield but to a cold back room in a funeral parlor and a trio of fresh graves in a rainswept cemetery. Sergeant Bolan came home to bury his mother, father, and teen-aged sister—and to arrange care for the only survivor of that tragedy at home, young brother Johnny.

Mack Bolan never "came home."

Rather, the Executioner merely shifted the focus of his war effort—retiring from the pointless and impersonal brutalities of those distant battle zones to wage the greater war at home. It was not the spirit of vengeance that sent the one-man army exploding into the ranks of the organized American underworld; it was, rather, a simple recognition that the savages were taking over the civilized world, and that something needed to be done about that.

Mack Bolan was uniquely qualified to do something. To know the man is to understand that, for him, there were no alternatives to the course he chose. To Bolan, his war against the Mafia was not a crusade but the minimum discharge of a maximum responsibility. He had the training, the tools, the desire, and the capability to "do something" as perhaps no other man alive could.

The decision was no decision at all.

It was simply a conditioned response by a trained warrior in the discharge of duty.

Bolan "did it" to them in Pittsfield, then in California, Arizona, Florida—even in France and England—and by the time he began pounding the "five family" New York area the entire world of Mafia knew that this guy had come to play the game as the game had never before been played.

He went on playing it, in the face of desperate countermeasures by "the enemy" and police establishments alike—growing into his destiny and rising constantly to each higher challenge along the warpath.

Bolan had never expected to live so long. It was a suicidal war, and he knew it—had known it from the beginning. Certainly he would not have remained alive beyond the first few skirmishes with this "omnipotent" enemy had he not continued to grow and to profit from his experiences. To say that the grim-eyed man who quietly invaded the mile-high country of Colorado one cool evening was precisely the same young warrior who, a couple of dozen campaigns earlier, had returned from the Asian war zones to bury his own beloved dead could be a fatal mistake for those who say it.

This was, sure, the same Mack Bolan—the Executioner, the one-man army, the war machine.

But he was more than that now.

Quite a bit more.

This purposeful young man had become a *superb* war machine.

There were those in Colorado who soon would be saying that he was some kind of superman. Perhaps that was true and perhaps it was not. Bolan himself would scoff at such an idea. But he would have reason to wish it were true.

He was invading a carefully prepared Kill Zone. Theirs, not his. The target was Bolan. All the power and resources of this seemingly omnipotent and infinite enemy were concentrated into this time and place, coiled and waiting, geared to an all-consuming determination to write a final end to Mack Bolan's war.

"I am both ready to die and willing to kill," Bolan had once declared.

Colorado would provide the ultimate test of that, and of the man himself.

Superman, no, not in the popular meaning of the word. Bolan bled like other men, knew pain and fear like other men—he would one day die like other men.

A *superb* man, yes, in every sense of that word.

In the Kill Zone they watched and waited for a superman. And there were those who thought for sure that they had found one . . . while others suspected that, instead, *he* had found *them.* As, indeed, he had.

1: SHOW OF ARMS

The Colorado bloodbath erupted at about dusk, on the eastern slope of the Rockies between Golden and Boulder.

A few minutes earlier, Bolan had left the main highway to slowly cruise Golden, out past the School of Mines, and onto the two-lane blacktop which links the two college towns.

It was, he knew, an invitation to combat—that maneuver.

They had been tracking him all the way from Denver, just hanging loose and awaiting an opportunity to close for the kill. The twenty-seven-foot GMC motor home was not a difficult target to follow, and Bolan had no illusions as to his ability to shake the pursuers—nor, indeed, did he wish to.

Leo Turrin's worried caution rippled the surface of his mind as he left the outskirts of Golden behind him: "It's a supersoft operation out there, Sarge. All I can get is odors, no intel at all. If you go, for God's sake hold your ass with both hands."

But, no, the man from blood did not wish to shake his pursuers. He had, in fact, taken particular pains to reveal his presence in the midst of that "supersoft" operation. Ten patient days of quiet probing had yielded nothing of significance to add to Leo's "odors," so Bolan had used the only option available.

He'd allowed *them* to see *him.*

An open probe of Denver's "strip," Colfax avenue—a few indiscreet questions, here and there—and yeah, like clockwork, there were the hounds of hell sniffing cautiously along his backtrack.

So okay. It was what he wanted. And he'd led them deliberately away from the urban sprawl of Denver and into an area with combat stretch. Not that Bolan was simply spoiling for a fight with this mile-high arm of the mob; he was still seeking intelligence, an angle into the "supersoft."

Now, though, he was beginning to wonder about the wisdom of that strategy. It had been a discreet tail, all the way to Golden. Then, suddenly, all discretion had gone to hell. The warwagon's radio scans had locked onto a *military* frequency in the VHF spectrum, and the console monitors were rattling continually with a barrage of urgent instructions issuing from some central "command" for the deployment of "killers."

"Killer Five from Command, assume Delta One."

"Roger, Command, Killer Five assuming Delta One."

"Killer Two, give me a short count for radio fix!"

"Command from Scout One! Bandit is tracking north on niner-three!"

"Roger, Scout One! All Killers, scramble order! Close on Scout One, tracking north on niner-three from Point Delta!"

So there it was.

"Niner-three" was the two-lane blacktop running north from Golden.

"Point Delta" had to be Golden.

And Bolan knew that game plan. Someone with a military mind was running this "hunt and kill" mission. For one long and terrible moment, Bolan had to consider the inconceivable: could this be an actual military operation? Could the U.S. Army be out here on a hunt-and-kill against Mack Bolan? The answer to that was swift and positive: of course it could be! Bolan was, after all, one of theirs—officially listed a deserter. But that answer simply did not compute. Those "scout cars" were Mafia crew wagons—and the people in them were street soldiers—torpedoes—not U.S. Army soldiers.

It was, however, highly important that Bolan know the enemy. He did not engage in military duels with soldiers of the same side—no matter what their mission might be. It was another time to be thankful for the "special systems" built into the warwagon. He activated the optic scanners and remoted the display to the forward console, instantly acquiring a blurred telescopic image of the following vehicle. The "optic-lock" responded to Bolan's command with a refinement of focus and a steady picture. The distance-measuring readout was indicating 400 meters—about a quarter-mile—and, yeah, it was the same vehicle he'd picked up on West Colfax—a big shiny Detroit black, fully crewed, armored—a crew wagon for damned sure.

His own speed had dropped to about 30mph as he fragged out his consciousness to cover all the needs of the moment—proper attention to navigation, surveillance of that chase car, intellectual assessment of the situation. The chase vehicle had slowed accordingly, maintaining the gap. He brought them closer, via the space-age optics, until the windshield of that heavy limousine filled the viewscreen of his console. Then he sent a command to the infra-red "augmentation" unit. The screen took on a ghastly reddish glow while the interior of that vehicle 400 meters to the rear became illuminated with invisible light to offer further secrets.

It was a positive make. No further doubts remained for the combat mind. The jump-seat limousine contained six scowling men, two in each seat row. Heavy weapons were in open display. The guy beside the driver was one Jingo Morelli, a cool operator out of Cleveland.

Bolan switched off the optics and punched in a geo-plot, consulting an automated index for the micro-frame desired then calling up the display for the area he was then traveling.

According to the plot, the Executioner was in damned lonely country. Sparsely settled, rugged terrain, damned few intersecting roads. As for present traffic on Route 93, there was none. Route 72 intersected at about halfway to Boulder, stretching toward the higher country. But Bolan was now betting that at least two of those "killers" were sitting up there at that intersection, awaiting the turkey shoot.

It was obvious now. They'd sucked him. This was no hastily conceived reaction to a Bolan contact. These guys had been *waiting* for that contact—expecting it, wanting it, prepared for it. Bolan had long known, of course, that he would trip one of these wires, one day. As time wound on and the war pressures mounted, the inevitability of this moment had become more and more certain. He'd long ago begun to suspect each contact with this enemy as a possible suck plan—a whirlpool that would grab him at the first casual touch and drag him to the depths of hell.

So okay. This one was obviously it.

Colorado was a Kill Zone. That was the only logical answer to the "supersoft" high country maneuvers. A spider's web had been woven here, probably with strands reaching everywhere. Then the whispers had gone down to the jungle telegraph, whispers which were designed to reach the Executioner's listening posts—*soft* whispers intended only to incite the curiosity of a Mafia-buster—and they'd sat back and waited for him.

Okay.

The knowledge came as almost a sense of relief.

Like the end of a long jungle night preceding a dawn jump-off, the battle itself became a welcome relief from the pressures of expectation.

These guys wanted a fight, huh?

So okay.

Bolan activated all of the warwagon's combat systems and turned close attention to the geoplot. He was approaching a series of rolling hills, upraised fingers of the Rockies lying upon the edge of the high plains, as good a spot as any for the death stand.

He awaited the moment when the crest of a hill momentarily separated him from the chase car, then summoned forth every horse available within the powerful Toronado engine to send the warwagon leaping away in the downhill stretch. The Detroit Black blinked into view at the top of that hill just as Bolan dropped behind the next one, and he could sense the consternation back there. The radio monitor quickly confirmed that feeling.

"Command, this is Chase One! He's spotted us, I think. Running hard north, about four miles from the junction!"

"Stay with him, Chase One," came the cool response. *"All Killers, this is a go! Secondary units maintain station for reaction as required. Primaries close immediately! All units acknowledge!"*

Bolan was counting the "killers" as each in his proper turn acknowledged the kill order. Good radio discipline, yeah. Military precision, sure. And it was quite a field army that was assembling out here on the Rockies' eastern slope. By simple extrapolation, a hundred troops minimum—with possibly several times that number in a closer count.

But Mack Bolan had stopped counting.

The long jungle night had ended, and the warrior was ready to greet the dawn—at the edge of the world, or at least it seemed that way. He'd picked his spot in the spider's web, and now he was off the highway and plunging across open country, running along a splayed finger and aiming for a knuckle overlooking and commanding all behind him.

The edge of the world, sure—but it wasn't a jungle, and it was just the opposite of dawn. This was "big sky" country, with the snowcapped peaks backdropping the western edge and standing out with stark relief against the red skies of sunset. Off to the east lay green flatlands for as far as the eye could see, and from here the eye could see the median between night and day—the shadow zone way off beyond Denver where the direct sunrays lingered in retreat.

There would be no retreat here.

There would be confrontation and death here.

And Mack Bolan was ready . . . for both.

2: DEATH FORCE

Bolan's bold initiative had succeeded in maneuvering the enemy into open country where the warwagon's combat systems would find maximum effectiveness. There were no trees here, no structures—no obstructions and no cover of any type. They would have to come at him along the bare spine of the hill, in a steady climb. Moreover, with nightfall almost upon them, there would be no time for cute stratagems. The darkness would be kinder to the hunted than to the hunters. Behind him stood the beginning of the heavily forested slopes, wild country with dramatic topography and an infinite number of escape routes for a fleeing man.

Bolan was not fleeing, but the enemy could not be certain of that. If they meant to have him, then the burden was theirs to attack immediately. They would, he knew, do so.

And he was ready for them. The battle cruiser was heeled about with her bow to the only path of attack. All surveillance systems were operative. The roof-mounted rocket pods were raised, locked, and ready. Personal weapons and ready-belts were placed near the door in readiness for extra-vehicular activities.

The enemy, also, appeared ready. Their progress along the uneven terrain had been not quite as rapid as Bolan's and apparently there had been some indecision regarding tactics during those first few moments of Bolan's cross-country plunge. But now they had shored up their game plan and the movement had become entirely methodical.

The heavy crew wagon had proven unfit for this leg of the journey, evidenced by the unhappy complaint via Bolan's radio monitors: "Command, this is Scout One. We're out of it. That guy must have some kind of special suspension on that yacht."

"Roger, Scout One," was the crisp command response. "Assume rear plug and stand by for further assignment. Killer One—report!"

"Killer One, aye. We're okay. Target is headed for the timber line. He'll have to dump the vehicle there. We are closing with all speed."

"Belay that!" the command voice instantly replied. "Advance with extreme caution only!" Then had followed a flurry of signals for positioning of units and coordination of the attack plan. Bolan counted five "killer" mobile units assembling down there while he finalized his own preparations for the battle—and when they came, it was straight out of the military book.

An apprehensive chill chased along his spine

and once again doubt surfaced in the combat mind as the warrior scanned that enemy force through the high resolution focal fields of the optics system. Five vehicles, yeah—army field vehicles, dammit, done up in the traditional OD colors—troop carriers, grinding slowly along that gradual incline in a well-spaced formation, with squads of infantry advancing cautiously behind them, very authentic-looking infantry wearing combat fatigues and carrying very familiar weapons.

Hell—it could not be!

Bolan fought himself through an agonizing moment of inner conflict, then he sent his own powerful radio transmitter clicking toward the VHF military channel under monitor. His voice was cold and militarily precise as he spoke into the microphone. "Command Radio, authentication check. Identify your unit and authorization code for use of this radio channel."

He counted off ten seconds before the response crackled through his monitor: "Roger, Circuit Control. Colorado Guard, Arapahoe Training Area. Field exercise in progress."

"Authenticate!" Bolan snapped.

"Roger. Stand by."

The VHF scanner immediately whirred and locked in to a terse command via that spectrum. "All units from Killer Command. Abandon communications primary—repeat—abandon primary. All further communications via this channel."

Bolan grinned soberly, all doubts again dissolved. So it was all a cover. Those were not real troops down there. But they were going to damn soon feel that they were.

He "enabled" the rocketry, an electronic command which automatically combined the optics with the fire control system, superimposing an electronic grid with rangemarks on the viewscreen.

The *Fire Enable* signal began pulsing.

Targeting was entirely via electronic circuitry, foot-controlled and fired from a floor-mounted device which Bolan described as "a rock and press track/fire." A supple ankle and steady foot were the chief requirements for this system. The launcher itself was built into the roof of the vehicle—a four-rocket pod which was normally retracted below a sliding roof panel for concealment. It was quickly raised and locked into the firing mode upon command.

The leading troop carrier was now centered in the range marks on Bolan's viewscreen. He locked in the tracking system, receiving a *Target Acquisition* red glow on the screen, then banged his knee with a fist to send the hot bird streaking away from the roof. The horizontal column of fire sizzled across that short range and instantly erupted into a blinding ball of roiling flames and dense smoke, totally obscuring the target area momentarily as the thunderclap shook the air and staggered the very earth beneath it. Mangled bodies and dazed faces appeared briefly on the viewscreen as Bolan corrected left and again banged his knee. Another vehicle went into dramatic destruct and spread its parts about the battlefield as an awed voice with no military precision whatever gasped into the UHF monitor: "My God! Get those people out of there!"

"Belay that!" snapped another, the voice of command. "Standard infantry deployment! Move 'em out and get 'em down!"

Bolan sent them a third whizzer, this one impacting on the nose of a big carrier which had become trapped in the wreckage of the first two. He then disabled the rocketry—saving that final round for another moment—and quickly prepared for EVA. The initiative was his, for the moment, and he knew that his only hope lay in a manipulation of that confusion down there—to keep hitting them with hellfire and thunderation so that their stunned senses could have no chance to get it back together, to regroup, to reform the attack.

He had them reeling, and he knew it—and he knew that he had to keep them that way.

Hardly before the shockwave from that third rocket had dissipated, the magnificent warrior had draped a readybelt across each shoulder, thumbed a high explosive fragmentation round into the waiting M-79, and ventured forth into the deepening dusk of that Colorado mountainside.

A mere thirty seconds of warfare, and already the battlefield was battered and groaning, traumatized by the brooding atmosphere of doom—terrorized by the hopeless cries of the dying and horrified by the shocking stillness of the dead.

Even so, it was a superior force awaiting him out there. He hadn't a chance of bulling his way through—and this much became immediately obvious. They had good leadership and they were playing it cool—quickly regrouping into small teams, going to ground and staying there, waiting him out.

One thing, at least, had been accomplished by the rocket attack. He'd cleared the spine area of the ridge. Nothing was up there, now, but the blazing wrecks of the three vehicles and the scattered dead. The other two troop carriers had plunged down the side of the ridge, and it would take some fancy maneuvering just to get them topside again. The foot soldiers had taken cover on both slopes; few were even in a position to return fire, and these few were obviously loathe to call attention to their positions.

The night was coming on suddenly, also—a characteristic of the eastern slopes of high mountain ranges. On the dark side of mountains, he recalled, gray dusk often goes to blackest night in a fingersnap—and that very thing appeared to be occurring here, now.

All of which gave Bolan pause to rethink his situation. The combat pause was a very brief one—a mere heartbeat of pause—and then he was flowing into a conditioned response to the survival instinct, taking maximum cover available and paying out the loads from the ready-belts, arranging the M-79 rounds on the ground beside him in a newly planned firing sequence. The idea, now, was not to decimate the enemy before they finally got to him—the idea was to keep living.

There was a slot down there—about fifty feet wide and two hundred feet long—a little chunk of no-man's-land which stood between entrapment and freedom, a slot which Bolan intended to neutralize completely.

When the M-79 began sending, the pattern was designed to obscure that slot to the maximum extent possible and also to keep it a highly unpopular zone. He was varying the rounds in a methodical sequence—high explosive, then gas, then smoke and repeating the sequence as he shoe-strung the pattern back and forth along the fire zone.

The barrage consumed about two minutes, and carried him into the anticipated sudden blackness of nightfall. Additionally, an acrid mixture of gas and smoke now overhung that slot in a suffocating cloud which obviously was also seeping down the slopes on either side, as evidenced by the fits of coughing and scurrying about in that area. At the slot's dead center, the burning wreckage from the rocket salvo glowed feebly through the pall, serving as a beacon in the gloom.

Bolan quickly returned to his vehicle and sent her rolling silently forward into the combat zone, without lights and without power, coasting in neutral and navigating by the muffled light of his own fires, gradually picking up speed through the hundred yards or so of quickening descent.

He was moving smartly through the slot before the sidelined enemy became aware of the maneuver, and there simply was no reaction possible, at that late moment. A futile volley of untargeted rifle fire was their only response, with Bolan already clear and rolling free toward the "rear plug"—that armored Detroit Black with a nervous crew of six hot guns.

Bolan slipped the warwagon into gear and brought the power in but left the normal lighting extinguished, bringing up instead the infra-red optics for instrument navigation.

The UHF command frequency was at that moment advising the plug vehicle of the situation. "It appears that our bandit broke out," clipped the cool voice. "Suggest you stand clear and let him pass. He has some kind of crazy firepower on that bus. Give him room and let him run but keep him in sight."

"Scout One—roger, understand."

Bolan, also, understood. And his "crazy firepower" already had the rear plug in its rangemarks.

He banged his knee just as the armor-plated vehicle began a slow movement to starboard in an apparent attempt to "stand clear."

The sizzling missile lifted away and roared along the firetrack in a hot intercept. The entire vehicle was enveloped in the fireball. It was punched around in a complete cartwheel then flipped onto its side, mortally wounded but saved from total disintegration by the protective steel plates.

Two guys were crawling clear of the smoking Cadillac when Bolan's vehicle reached the scene. Both were bloodied and dazed, but one of them raised a pistol and waved it drunkenly at Bolan as he stepped from the warwagon.

Bolan blew the guy away with a hipshot from the .44 AutoMag. The other one was the man from Cleveland, Jingo Morelli.

"Kiss your ass goodbye, Jingo," Bolan icily advised him.

The guy was not all that dazed. He fell onto his back and showed the man from blood empty hands and pleading eyes. "Hey man—don't do it."

Bolan dropped a death medal onto that frozen chest. "Give me one reason why I shouldn't, guy."

Those doomed eyes rolled toward hope. "Uh—anything. Say it. Anything."

"Who's your boss?"

"Uh—God, I dunno. Wait! Now wait! Give me time to lay it out! I—"

"I didn't ask for a layout," Bolan coldly reminded him. "It's now or never, Jingo."

"Hey, we never see the guy. God's truth. He's not one of us—that's all I know."

Bolan understood that but he wanted the guy to say it, flat and straight. "It's a dumb time for double talk," said the voice of death.

"I swear! He's a contractor. From outside somewhere. Those soldier boys are his, not ours."

"So what are you doing here, Jingo?"

"Advisors, that's all. They needed someone to finger you. I didn't ask for the crummy job, Bolan. I don't even like the—listen, this guy is an operator. Read me?—an operator! He's working for the million bucks head money plus full expenses. He's got a whole fuckin' army stashed around here somewheres. I mean all of it. Troops, weapons, vehicles. We call him the little general."

It was all very interesting, much more than Bolan had expected to get. "What else do you call him, Jingo?"

"I swear I don't know his name!"

The AutoMag came up to stare the guy squarely in the eyes. "Kiss it goodbye, then, Jingo."

"Okay, okay," Morelli sighed. "He's got a code name. They call him Trooper. Now that's the all of it, I swear. I never seen the guy. I don't know nobody that did. The contact is always by telephone or radio. He's got a secret base up here, somewhere. He runs everything from there."

"So who was running *this* hit?"

"*He* was. By radio. I swear."

Bolan's numbers had run out. Already too much time had been spent here, at the edge of the death zone.

"Tell him I've come for him, Jingo. Tell him I got his message. Tell him."

The guy could hardly believe his good fortune. Relief flooded the voice with emotion as he replied, "Sure, sure, I'll tell 'im, Bolan."

"Don't move a muscle until I'm clear," Bolan commanded.

He returned to the warwagon and went on, without lights, to the highway.

But the Executioner was not now "running hard" anywhere.

He pulled on across the highway and into thick brush, then returned to the roadway to erase any tracks or signs left there. Moments later, and long before the remnants of the "killer force" began their quiet withdrawal, all of the warwagon's surveillance systems were fully operational—reading and waiting for directions to the next front.

The game had changed. There was now no clear distinction between the hunter and the hunted. And the entire "kill zone" was now no-man's-land.

3: COLD

A very bold mind was running that operation.

Sharply uniformed troops with MP armbands stood guard over the entrance to the battlefield while work parties and graves details picked the area clean of every evidence of combat. Large, flatbed semitrailers hauled away the gutted hulks and incidental pieces of the shattered troop carriers while field ambulances carted off the dead and broken bodies and medics provided first aid to the walking wounded. Even a wrecker showed up to tow away the remains of the armored Cadillac.

Bolan maintained his surveillance throughout that cleanup operation, recording the terse radio communiqués, photographing faces and equipment with infra-red techniques, monitoring personal conversations with his sensitive audio pickups.

And, yeah, it was quite an operation.

Too much, perhaps, for too little. Bolan simply could not believe that such a formidable force had been organized for the sole purpose of stopping the Executioner's war.

There had to be more to it than that.

These guys were operating openly, brazenly—masquerading as a bona fide U.S. military force, utilizing restricted radio channels for their communications, riding around in "official" vehicles and arming themselves with modern weaponry from the U.S. arsenal—and the hell of it all was that they were pulling it off flawlessly. Observers from the Joint Chiefs of Staff would not have detected a suspicious anomaly.

All this . . . for one lone man?

The financial considerations alone were staggering. Even supposing that they'd managed to steal all the equipment, weapons, and ammunition, the day-to-day cost of maintaining such a force would be immense.

Dark suspicions were lurking at the threshold of the combat mind as Bolan tailed the last of the column away from there. The track led north and then west, deeper into the mountains in a torturous and winding ascent which seemed to be holding a general northwest focus. The final few miles were accomplished via a succession of narrow roads and back trails which culminated in a swift descent along a broad, freshly paved private road which dipped into an almost pastoral valley, high between snowcapped peaks.

Bolan had endeavored to maintain a track-plot, but he was not at all certain as to the precise geographic location of this "base."

The air was very thin, and quite cold—rare enough to noticeably impair the efficiency of the warwagon's engine. The stars had never seemed brighter, the sky closer.

Bolan broke off the track at the beginning of that final descent and pulled into cover at about two hundred yards above the base. A high chain-link fence was set behind barbed-wire escarpments. A large sign at the gate identified the enclosure only as "U.S. Government Property." A pair of MP's closed the gate behind the last vehicle of the column and returned to an All Terrain Vehicle which was parked at the approach, serving apparently as a guard house. Considerable activity was going on behind that fence—a lot of lights, vehicles whining around, a miscellany of muffled sounds. Apparently, though, the main area was nestled into the base of the mountain slope and at a right angle to Bolan's line of sight; he could see nothing in the nature of buildings or organized human activity.

In preparation for an EVA, he stripped down to the blacksuit, briefly debated the mission requirements, then removed that also and put on a "life suit"—a lightweight jumpsuit which maintains body temperature within the comfort level. Over this he added the usual "light probe" gear—9mm Beretta Brigadier with silencer, a high-powered air pistol with tranquilizer darts, stiletto, nylon garrote, various gadgets. Then he applied a black cosmetic to face and hands and quietly invaded the night.

The temperature down on the plains had been in the mid-fifties; here, it was closer to the freezing mark. Occasional light patches of old snow created patchwork patterns on the landscape. Light sagebrush shared the dotted valley floor with a thin scattering of small pines. Erratic gusts of wind moaned fleetingly along the soft terrain and sometimes howled against the rocks, somewhere above.

Bolan blended with all that, became one with it, absorbing it while himself becoming absorbed by it as he moved off in a quiet reconnaissance.

He followed the fence line, at a distance of about fifty yards, pausing frequently to watch and listen, quiveringly alert to any suggestion of the presence of land mines, trip wires, and other silent security provisions. It was not a huge base. He covered the entire open perimeter area in less than twenty minutes, completing the "close recon," then withdrew for a quicker transit along the base of the opposite slope, in an open reconnaissance of the entire valley.

Not large, no—but a hell of a neat setup.

The topography here seemed to suggest a moraine area—the melting point of some ancient glacier—with the secret base situated between a pair of lateral moraines with peculiar angles. The rear area was butted into the mountainside, two sides protected by the moraines, only the front boundary unobscured by natural terrain features. Because of the rise and angles of the land, the whole thing was shuttered from the view of casual passersby—probably even from above—except for a line of sight covering no more than fifteen degrees of arc.

They apparently felt pretty damn secure in there.

No guards were posted, except at the gate. The fence was electrified, though, and there was evidence to suggest that perhaps some sort of electronic alarm system was functioning.

Bolan sat on a rock in the shadow of a scrubby

pine and sketched the layout. Fifteen medium-sized quonset huts—each capable of housing, probably, twenty to thirty men, depending on how much they wanted to crowd it. Large motor pool area with plenty of rolling stock. A central, low-profile building—probably a mess and lounge area—now serving coffee and sandwiches to a subdued "killer force" who gathered in apathetic groups outside. Smaller building with an Alpine roof, set off from the other structures—headquarters, probably—brightly lighted inside, much bustling about. A small shack, off to the other side—infirmary, judging by the activities there. Couple of large metal warehouses, a miscellany of smaller storage sheds.

Nice setup, yeah.

Bolan completed the sketch and carefully put it away for safekeeping. Then he settled into a quiet vigil, eyes and ears alert to all the lifesigns in and about that incredible encampment in the Rockies. Two hours passed before the patient scout was satisfied that he "knew" the place—had its heartbeat, its rhythms, its very metabolism.

The facts, however, still did not compute. It was too damn much for much too little; Bolan simply could not buy this full-scale military operation as nothing more than a headhunting force. They'd gone for *his* head, sure—but there had to be more to it than that.

Jingo Morelli had tried to make it sound like a head force—*He's working for the million bucks head money plus full expenses*—but he'd also referred to the top man as an "independent contractor," a situation which could cover a variety of bold ideas.

"Full expenses," for an operation such as this

one, would make peanuts of the million-dollar bounty on Bolan's head. Was the mob really financing the entire thing? Bolan's dark suspicions would not leave him. Something was out of whack here.

Was it possible that the mob was playing footsy with some official government agency, a *furtive* agency, perhaps?

Possible, sure—anything was possible.

Lucky Luciano had been let out of prison by an official government agency, to run the New York docks during the scarey days of World War Two.

The mob and the CIA had gotten chummy in the face of Castro's Cuba, and it was no secret that "the boys" had lately managed to forge friendships in the shadow of the White House itself.

No, nothing was impossible.

Bolan was preparing to break off the reconnaissance and return to the warwagon when another piece of the puzzle suddenly fell from the skies—literally. The unmistakable windmill sounds of a small helicopter froze him to the shadows, and he watched as the little bird dropped quickly from the peak behind him and settled into the compound. The angle of vision into the landing area was a bad one; Bolan had only a sensing of shadowy figures moving quickly about the grounded craft—whether embarking or debarking, he could not say—then the chopper was lifting away, with less than a minute on the ground.

The chopper itself held the most interest for Bolan.

It carried U.S. Army markings.

He made a thoughtful mental note of that as he

began the withdrawal. It was a cold withdrawal—*inside* cold—as the most hunted man in America began to assimilate the full implications of his situation.

He knew that he had to face the possibilities squarely. Regardless of who was calling the shots, those "troops" down there *could* be U.S. Army soldiers. This *could* be a "friendly" force, subverted by those above them into the counterwar against Mack Bolan.

And, yes, it was a chilling thought.

Bolan had always made it a point to confine his war to the proper enemy. He had never shot it out with cops or other officials; he simply evaded them, the best way he could.

But, now . . .

Yes, it was a cold withdrawal for the Executioner. Already he had engaged this present "enemy" and left many dead upon the field of combat. And there was no way Bolan could rationalize an "error" of that magnitude.

No way.

If he was getting that sloppy—if his combat instincts had gone that sour—then it was time for the war to end.

How could he ever again trust himself with the death decision? An executioner's "error" was noncorrectable.

Dammit—he had to *know!*

The troubled warrior cautiously circled to the access road and invested another ten quiet minutes in a study of the gate area. The all-terrain vehicle had not budged from its earlier position. The gate guard, two "soldiers" in white MP helmets, maintained their lonely vigil from inside the vehicle. Automatic weapons stood at the ready.

Bolan settled into the wait, patiently determined to find the truth about this place. The ten minutes seemed like hours, and he was ready for the "MP" who finally stepped down from the guard vehicle. The guy left his weapon on the seat, did a couple of quick deep knee bends, muttered something to his companion and lit a cigarette, then ambled into the sagebrush at the edge of the road.

It was the moment Bolan had been waiting for.

He moved swiftly then, along the blind side of the vehicle until he was about ten paces out, where he raised the air pistol and sent a stun-dart to the guy in the vehicle. The guy raised a hand to the back of his neck and quietly collapsed. That dart would very quickly dissolve. Within thirty minutes to an hour, depending on the guy, the drug itself would vanish entirely from the bloodstream. The guy would awaken as though from a normal nap and all the tests known to medical science would fail to reveal the cause of it all.

Bolan waited for the second man to return from his "head call"—then he soft-touched him, also, dropping the guy in mid-stride. He carried him to the vehicle and placed him on the seat beside the other one, then began the quick shakedown.

Both wore dog tags—official army ID tags. Bolan took impressions of each, using the pencil-and-paper technique for blocking-in the raised lettering. He found other useful information in pockets and wallets, making notes of these items.

Finally he copied the serial numbers from the automatic weapons and from the vehicle itself.

When he returned to the warwagon a few minutes later, there was nothing left behind to suggest his visit. Those guys would awaken feeling just a bit groggy, perhaps a bit disoriented for a couple of minutes—and probably neither would admit to the other that he'd actually been asleep.

But as the warwagon quietly powered away from that cold zone, Bolan was now almost dead certain that he had made a horrendous error in judgment.

And the coldness went with him, seeping into his chest and burying itself there. They'd finally done it to him. They'd sucked him, set him up—and now, maybe, he was no different than they.

That was cold, yeah—bitter cold.

4: CRACKER

Harold Brognola occupied the most sensitive chair in Washington. He was unofficially referred to as "the nation's No. 2 cop"—denoting his position in the U.S. Department of Justice. With all the recent hysteria surrounding that city, he'd also found himself plugged into the hotseat as "special advisor" on the National Security Council. As if that were not enough, he was also the man with the federal charter to stop the illegal crusade of one Mack Bolan.

In his essentials, Brognola was actually an organized crime specialist. He had been far down in the ranks, as leader of a federal organized crime task force, when Sgt. Bolan returned from Vietnam and began slugging it out with the enemy on the home turf. Being an absolute realist, the federal cop had immediately recognized the effectiveness of Bolan's illegal war and he'd moved quickly to secretly align himself—and thus his government—with that effort. Bolan himself had never been too happy nor even comfortable with any such arrangement, even though, early during the wars, Brognola had managed to arm-twist official secret sympathy for the guy in Washington. It was during the fourth major campaign that Brognola carried to the warrior a full package "deal"—including general amnesty and a pledge of quiet government support of the war. All they'd wanted in return was a bit of control over the guy. But Bolan had turned it down flat.

The guy's guns were not for hire.

"Thanks," he'd quietly told Brognola, "but I don't want a license."

Brognola understood. And it deepened the admiration he held for the big cool guy. But it sure made Brognola's job tougher. With that refusal to join forces came the end of the brief romance from Washington. The reaction was swift and imperative. *Stop the guy.* And, of course, Brognola was given the grim assignment.

He'd been walking a tightwire ever since.

Mack Bolan was like a magic hen who lays golden eggs. All you had to do was follow the guy around and pick up the pieces in his wake. Brognola had been doing just that, and the official war on organized crime was benefitting in every way. Brognola himself had fallen heir to considerable personal benefits. What the hell—he'd gone clear to the No. 2 spot, thanks in large part to the one and only Mack Bolan.

And the big brass wanted that hen *dead?*

Harold Brognola was a cop, sure, a good cop, but he was also a human being. He did not want Mack Bolan dead—nor even removed from circulation. It was a tightwire act, but Hal Brognola remained committed to a friendship and to a human relationship that transcended professional ethics. He remained committed to Mack Bolan.

And so did another. Leo Turrin would stand up to God himself, on Bolan's behalf. Leo was a No. 2 man, also—on the other side. Underboss in the mob's Pittsfield arm, he was the highest ranked *mafioso* ever to carry a secret federal badge. The undercover cop from Pittsfield had been an obscure underling in the syndicate when Bolan started ripping them up. He would have ripped Leo, as well—and came uncomfortably close to doing just that before the little guy revealed his true role to Bolan. Leo Turrin had since led a triple life—federal agent, mafia boss, Bolan ally. The two fed each other, and the interchange had been as profitable for one as for the other. Turrin's rise in mob circles were meteoric. His federal stock had reaped huge dividends, as well. The value of the spin-off there was incalculable—and none was more aware of this than Hal Brognola. Very soon, it was felt, Turrin would be joining the elite circle of syndicate power known as *La Commissione*—the official ruling body of the organized underworld. No price could be too high for an undercover seat in that circle.

And, no, Brognola did not want Mack Bolan dead or even disabled.

Nor did Leo Turrin.

The call came in the grayness of a Washington dawn.

"This is Sticker," announced the familiarly disguised voice from Pittsfield.

"Just a minute," Brognola growled, and switched to the hold line. "Business," he mumbled to the sleepy inquiry in his wife's eyes as he left the bed. He lit a cigar and pulled on a robe, in that order, then went directly to the study where he diverted the call into a security hookup.

"Okay, Sticker. Who dies at dawn?"

"Depends," was the quiet reply. "What's going in Colorado?"

Brognola sighed. "Many things. The Broncos are looking good this year. Could even make it to the play-offs. I hear also happy reports from Aspen—should be a good year for skiing. Other than that, who knows about Colorado?"

"You should," Turrin told him. "They're calling Denver the left bank of Washington. Just because we have an athlete in the White House these days is no reason to downgrade all the rest."

"Okay, sure. Colorado is Government West. So what? For a conversation at dawn, tell me—so the hell what?"

"So Striker's out there, that's what. Only this time he appears to be the struckee. The guy's in a hell of a sweat, Hal. Wants to know if there's a federal game plan running there. Says he's encountered a quote military killer force unquote. He inflicted heavy casualties in the breakaway. Thought they were quote enemy forces unquote. But now he's sweating the sweats of the damned. Frankly, so am I. I'm the one put him onto the area."

"You had movements?"

"Well . . . sort of. Odors more than movements. Striker smells a setup. He has positive make on one faction. They are mine, and that's a positive. The others, he has reasons to believe, are yours. A combination, Hal. Are you running one?"

"No."

"That didn't sound like a hundred percent *no.* Are you on top of the question?"

"I guess not. To my knowledge, it's a no. I'll have to look around. Did you say heavy casualties?"

Turrin sighed sibilantly into the connection. "Yeah."

"Dammit."

"Well . . . I guess it had to happen. It's hard to call the players without a program, Hal. I don't know how the guy has managed to do it, all this time. The point is—you know what a conscientious whitehat the guy is—the point is this: the guy has been on the edge for a long time. He's not a psychopath, you know, and—"

Brognola snorted into that line of reasoning. "Of course he's not. He's the sanest man I ever—"

"Okay, that's just the point. If it turns out that he's slaughtered a bunch of his 'soldiers of the same side,' then you know what that's liable to do to the guy. As I say, he's been on the edge. An ordinary man would have cracked long ago. This could be *his* cracker, Hal. Frankly, I'm worried to death."

Brognola chewed that for a moment before replying, "So am I, Sticker. Listen, I want to talk to him. Tell him to contact me."

"You know he won't do that," Turrin said. "He is, though, sending you a package. Contains names and army serial numbers, also identification numbers off of some weapons and a military vehicle, some fingerprints, photographs, various items of intelligence. Wants you to put it together. I'll be calling you again in exactly four hours. And I hope to God, Hal, that you'll have some comforting words I can pass on to the guy."

"Where do I get the package?"

"Meet TWA Flight 250, arriving Dulles at eight o'clock, registered parcel. It's addressed to Harold Brown."

"Okay," Brognola replied, sighing. "I'll get it. Meanwhile, you contact our shining knight and tell him to cool it until he hears from me in the matter. He's to go to ground and lay there. Make sure he understands that."

"He says he's in the web," Turrin gloomily reported. "Says another quote death decision unquote could confront him at any moment. But he's tied his own hands, Hal. And that's what worries me. You get me happy words, damn quick, so I can untie the guy."

"Goddammit, Goddammit," Brognola muttered as he hung up.

He returned to the bedroom and a fully awakened wife.

She told him, softly, "You look as though you'd just confronted your own id."

"Go back to sleep, Helen," he said, sighing, and began getting into his clothes.

"You're going out? This early? Without breakfast?"

"I'll pick up something on the way."

"On the way to where?" she wanted to know. Washington wives had become terribly edgy, of late. Helen Brognola was no exception. "What's going on?"

He pulled on his pants and made a face at his "bride" of twelve years. "Business," he replied quietly.

"Monkey business, I'll bet," she said, trying to mask her uneasiness with banter.

There was a "thing" between Hal Brognola and his bride—a sort of spooky, ESP-ish thing. She always knew.

He gave it to her in a single word. "Bolan."

"Oh," she said, eyes wide and fixed on his. "Is it bad?"

Helen had never met Mack Bolan, never set eyes on him. But she knew him. She knew him well, via that "thing" with her husband.

"It's bad," he told her.

"Give him our love," she whispered, as she kissed her husband goodbye.

Hal Brognola knew that Mack Bolan would need much more than that.

What the guy needed was a band of angels.

And not even the No. 2 cop of the nation could provide him with that.

5: THICKENINGS

At the time of gray dawn in Washington it remained a star-filled night over Colorado. It had been a busy night for Mack Bolan. Withdrawing from that secret base, he had carefully plotted the track and precisely fixed the geographic location in the general area of Mt. Audubon—just south of Rocky Mountain National Park and the Shadow Mountain Recreation Area, though well removed from any center of human activity. It was a very wild area of few roads and virtually no human habitation. The nearest town appeared to be a small mountain village called Peaceful Valley, and it was here that Bolan found himself at just past midnight. He found a campsite a few miles farther south, where he parked the warwagon and immediately began programming the intelligence gathered by her surveillance systems during that long stakeout in the shadow of Mt. Audubon.

Though there was a wealth of information stored in the surveillance banks, very little of it seemed to be of a useful nature—at the present stage of things, anyway. The infra-red photography seemed to hold the richest store but even that was no more than an assortment of anonymous faces and equipment.

The final reading from the program scans was no more than a subjective judgment verifying the misgivings gained first hand. The operation bore all the earmarks of U.S. Military, and there was simply nothing in the evidence to refute it. Bolan would not have engaged that force had it not been for the clear Mafia presence in their midst—and, of course, there was the klinker. The only true comfort to be found there, for Bolan, was the death's-edge testimony of Jingo Morelli, the hood from Cleveland. And even that small comfort was watered a bit by the possibility that Jingo himself could have been misled with regard to the true setup. Jingo was a nobody, a small timer without distinction in the enemy ranks. He would not necessarily know exactly what was happening in Colorado.

One thing did stand out clearly in the electronic intelligence data. The movement against Bolan had been well planned and carefully coordinated. Their only error was the one that beat them: a miscalculation of Bolan's firepower. The rocketry had come as a surprise. They had not been prepared for anything like that.

Next time, they would be.

Bolan's problem was to determine if there was to be a next time. He needed identification of that opposing force. Beyond that, he had no clear task in mind at the moment—there was simply the knowledge that he was in a hell of a cold situation regardless of which way that identity turned. He was in their web and he knew it. A certain amount of localized movement would be possible, but any attempt to break completely clear of the kill zone was almost certain to result in confrontation and engagement. It was not the sort of game Bolan preferred to play—not even when the sides were clearly identified and the tasks more or less defined. He did not know the precise perimeter of the kill zone. He did not know the full dimensions of the killer force. The Shadow Mountain base did not have to be the only one; there could be others. If that was *really* U.S. Army out there . . . ?

Yeah, it was a cold situation. Colder than anything he could imagine. It was equivalent to being in deep penetration of VC territory with the entire countryside aroused to your presence there and with the uncomforting suspicion that your own forces had been ordered to shoot you on sight.

This whole lousy war had been conducted under those conditions, of course. Things had been that way since the first shot, at Pittsfield. But with a difference. In those earlier situations, the enemy always wore civvies and the others carried police badges. It was possible to draw a line between the two forces and to confine the war to the true enemy. Bolan felt no enmity toward the cops and other legal authorities. They were simply upholding the law. By any standard of law, Bolan was wrong and they were right. Bolan understood that and accepted it. He also understood his own imperatives. He was not, in his own understanding, a criminal except in the sense that he evaded due process of law. He would not compromise that position, and he would not knowingly attack those who were simply discharging their duties under the law.

So, yeah, he was now in a crisis situation, and he knew it. If that was genuine U.S. Army out there, hunting his head in a bonafide government operation . . . well, okay, the war was probably over. He would use every available maneuver to slip clear of the kill zone without direct contact, but it seemed highly doubtful that he could succeed in that. Contact would very probably be made. And the war would end right there, at that point of contact.

So, yes, it was very important that he identify that killer force. He would not hand over his head to just anyone.

Such was the line of thought that sent Mack Bolan through those final hours of that dismal night in the Colorado high country.

As soon as the intelligence data had been reduced to its most usable form, he transferred a thoughtful selection of it to a small attaché case with a shoulder strap. Then he put on Levi's and a heavy woolen shirt, mountain boots, the Beretta shoulder rig, and a warm jacket. Finally he snugged-in the warwagon and activated the security system. The battle cruiser was, for the moment, a distinct liability. She would remain in the relatively safe harbor of the public campground for awhile. For wheels, he went from the sublime to the ridiculous: a tiny trailbike from the warwagon's cargo hold. Then he backtracked to

Pleasant Valley in search of wheels with a bit more stretch to them.

He located some at a gas station which was closed for the night—a battered Ford pickup with "4-Sale $375" scrawled across its windshield. He kicked the tires all around, then hotwired the ignition and got a decent response from the engine.

Satisfied that the ancient vehicle was good for at least a few more miles, Bolan made his "midnight purchase" via four hundred-dollar bills in an envelope taped to the door of the station. He stowed the trailbike in the bed of the pickup and once again headed south, returning to the war-wagon only to drop off the bike and to pick up some gas for the new wheels.

The descent to the high plains was uneventful, but at several points along the route to Denver he spotted "military" vehicles with alert occupants who scrutinized everything that moved past them. There were no challenges to the battered pickup truck, however, and this was a hopeful sign of the true situation. A legitimate force could have set up roadblocks. They would not necessarily do so, of course; many tactical considerations could discourage anything more than a soft watch. Still, the absence of roadblocks left the question open—and this was enough for Bolan, for the moment.

Stapleton Field, in Denver, presented an entirely different perspective, however. The place was crawling with cops. Nothing as obvious as roadblocks and physical searches—but they were there, and in force, in a typical high-priority surveillance network. Strands of the web cast for Mack Bolan? Maybe, yeah. If so, then the situation was thickening—perhaps hopelessly so.

Bolan donned a hunter's cap and wire-rimmed clear-lens glasses and went on into the web. If the mob were really working a combination on Bolan then they were finessing it to the fullest potential, ringing in every conceivable force which could be bent to their designs. And if that seemed too far out, then the alternative was almost as bad.

Traffic was light, and the parking areas around the main terminal practically devoid of movement. Bolan circled through, the battered vehicle drawing momentarily interested stares from the stake-outs. Again, however, no one challenged his presence there. He went on past the passenger terminal and parked in a waiting zone outside the air freight office, nodded to an airport security cop, and went inside.

The guy followed him in and watched with mild interest as Bolan filled out a shipping order for the attaché case.

"Make sure it gets on that three o'clock flight, eh."

"Five minutes more and you wouldn't have made it," the clerk replied.

"Yeah, I was sweating that." Bolan gazed deliberately at the security cop as he added, "What's all the excitement outside? I kept expecting someone to grab me. I wouldn't have made that flight, for sure. What's going on?"

The clerk chuckled and threw a quick glance at the airport cop. "Cops 'n' robbers," he said mildly. "Ask *him*."

Bolan did. "What the hell's going on?"

The guy rested a hand on the butt of the .38 and made a long face as he replied. "Looking for a fugitive." The tone of voice clearly implied that this was a routine matter, of little importance in the day-to-day intrigues in the life of an airport security officer.

The express clerk chuckled at that, also. "Probably a kid stole a car," he told Bolan as he accepted the money for the shipment.

The cop heard that and stepped closer to defend his profession. "Kid, hell," he said, lowering his voice to a confidential whisper. He was speaking to the clerk, primarily. "We got a tip that Mack Bolan is in the area. He'd better not try using this airport, I'll tell you."

The clerk, a white-haired man of about sixty, sniffed at that and went through a door with Bolan's shipment.

Bolan gazed at the cop through his clear lenses and mildly asked him, "Who's Mack Bolan?"

"Hell, where you been buried?" the cop growled. "He's the most-wanted fugitive in the country."

Bolan allowed his eyes to reveal how impressed he was with that tidbit. He muttered something appropriate and went back to his truck. The cop followed him outside, hand on gun, and watched him drive away.

A "tip," huh?

So, again, that could mean everything or nothing.

Bolan carefully withdrew from that thickening edge of the web and went in search of a public telephone. The intelligence package was on its way to "Harold Brown" in Washington. It would be a flight of about three hours. Meanwhile, he needed to contact Leo Turrin and apprise him of the Colorado situation.

After that . . . what?

A plan of action was forming behind the combat brow. Turrin and Brognola were good friends and comforting allies, sure, but their support of the Bolan effort was necessarily limited to quiet and more or less indirect activities—which meant, in the present situation, very little comfort to the man in the web.

It would be another three hours before Brognola could even begin to analyze the intelligence.

For a guy who was accustomed to living on the heartbeat, three hours could represent several lifetimes.

Bolan could not wait for his friends from the other side of the continent. He had to act *now*—had to do *something* to clarify the situation and perhaps weaken that web of containment which thickened at every touch.

So okay. First, contact Leo. Then, maybe, a strike at the heart of the web. That would be the only vulnerable point. But there lay the dilemma. Where was that heart?

He would have to probe for it.

But delicately. Yeah. Very, very delicately.

6: PERSPECTIVES

The Colorado dawn was anything but gray. It lit the eastern horizon of the plains with several shades of red and cast the westward mountains in profiles of stark black, with here and there a luminescently glowing snowcap luxuriating in the first oblique rays of the advancing sun. It was an awe-inspiring view, enough to remind a man of his mortality.

But Mack Bolan did not need the reminder.

Death was crowding his every heartbeat, and he knew it, as he abandoned the old truck at the edge of the southern suburban community of Cherry Hills and proceeded on foot toward the modest mansion of one Thomas Rizzi, one of the several low-profile mob figures of the area.

Besides the usual nickel-and-dime operations such as prostitution, gambling and so forth, it was also known that Rizzi was the money man behind a number of "legit" businesses in Denver and surrounding towns. He owned a local finance company, several restaurants and a couple of go-go joints on the west side, held a half-interest in a shopping center, and had lately began blossoming with a land promotion scheme in the Mancos area of Southwestern Colorado. Bolan had checked the guy out thoroughly as one of his first items of business upon arriving in Denver, and had dismissed him from the search for the "supersoft" in Colorado. Now, however, it seemed appropriate to take a closer look at the Rizzi operation. He may not be *part* of the supersoft, went the reasoning, but if other elements of the mob were in fact operating on Rizzi's turf, then the rules of the game prescribed the simple courtesy of at least informing the man of that other presence there.

Bolan intended to have a talk with the guy. Which could be risky enough, in itself. Escalating that risk was the obvious fact that others were expecting him to try it. Bolan had spotted two police cruisers quietly prowling the neighborhood as he made his initial pass through in the pickup truck. Another car, unmarked, was on stakeout in a driveway several houses east of the Rizzi mansion. Bolan read those vibes as cops, also. The "tip" must have gone down hard if the local cops were investing this kind of manpower; the deployment he'd encountered thus far in the city could mean nothing short of a full scale drag-net—most probably an area-wide alert, since several police jurisdictions seemed to be participating. Nevertheless, Bolan meant to have that parley with Tom Rizzi.

The only thing which Bolan seemed to have

working in his favor was an angle of possible overkill from the other side. Too many cooks were stirring the stew. Aside from the standard police set, some third force was present in that neighborhood—the supersoft, maybe?—a presence more felt than seen, something quiet and ominous overhanging that neighborhood like an atmosphere of doom. It was primarily a gut feeling, for Bolan, but he'd learned to trust his gut.

So now he was afoot, lightly armed, attired in the same mountaineering garb he'd worn down from Peaceful Valley, making a frontal approach on the target. Given all the circumstances, this was the best way. He could spring away in any direction at the lightest provocation—or, operating openly, seize and manipulate the unfolding events into a pattern of his own making.

It was an upper-crust residential district of fine homes and manicured grounds, here and there a walled estate, plenty of trees and shrubbery. The Rizzi place was not walled nor even fenced but stood in splendid isolation atop a grassy knoll, several hundred feet off the street—a colonial style structure with white columns and portico. A paved drive lined with young evergreens split the grounds at the center then formed an oval at the front of the house, passing beneath the portico and providing plenty of close parking. A three-car garage with overhead housing was set off to the side.

On Bolan's first pass of the morning, the place had been lit up from ground to roof. Four cars occupied the parking oval and another was parked in front of the garage. The police stakeout was across the street and three drives up, in excellent visual command of the situation. The officially marked cruisers prowled quietly on the perimeters, close enough for a quick response yet distant enough to not discourage a penetration of the area.

That other factor, the disturbing one, centered about a couple of casual anomalies which only finely tuned instincts would detect. One of those was a home-delivery milk truck which seemed to be spending far too much time in the area. Milkmen had to be hustlers if they meant to make a living. They had large routes to cover, and they had to "drop and git" if they were to drop it all in the prescribed time. This guy had been fifteen minutes in one residential block of single-unit dwellings. So, chalk up one for the gut.

Minutes before the milkman made the scene, a guy had spent too much time delivering newspapers from a panel truck.

And, now, one block north, a telephone company truck was dawdling at a pole while the "repairman" walked inane circles around its base. Ma Bell efficiency . . . at *dawn?*

Gut stuff, sure—but that was the stuff of life and death for a guy like Mack Bolan. Those people could, of course, be cops themselves. But it all seemed a bit much for a routine stake-out. If the cops were really dragging the area and trying to cover all possibilities, they'd never get the job done with a spread so thick.

Bolan strode straight along the street at dead center, looking neither left nor right, past the parked milk truck and on another hundred yards or so to the police stake-out vehicle. He halted abruptly at that point, went to the curb and sat on it, his back to the vehicle, and tiredly massaged the calves of his legs.

"You guys have the easy detail," he said in a conversational tone, without looking around.

"Don't bet on it," replied a bored voice from the vehicle. "What's up?"

"Daybreak, that's what," Bolan said, matching the other's bored tone. "The guy isn't going to show."

"Don't bet on that, either. Do I know you?"

"I hope not," Bolan replied casually. "It's not exactly my job to be known by guys like you. You been watching that milkman?"

A brief pause, then the quiet reply: "Yeah, off and on."

"Been here quite a while."

"Well, you know what they say about milkmen."

"Not this one. Spends most of his time in the truck. Better check him out."

"He's not, uh, one of your beards?"

"He's not one of mine," Bolan assured the cop. "Also there's a telephone lineman just around the corner up there."

"So?"

"So did you ever get a phone fixed in the middle of the night?"

The voice behind him sighed. A moment later, Bolan heard the subdued squawking of a radio conversation. He stood up and brushed off the seat of his pants.

"Okay, we're checking them out," the stakeout voice advised him.

Bolan nodded curtly and walked on. So far, so good. And it was no discredit to those cops that they'd played Bolan's game. They were programmed for it, victims of the grim quiet games they play among themselves along the twisted jungle paths which had become the law enforcement game.

It was, sure, hard to tell the players without a program. Luckily for Bolan, that truth applied equally to both sides. And it was not all luck. It was, indeed, 1 percent luck and 99 percent pluck. The hell of it was, you had to spend all the pluck before falling back upon that luck percentage—and then, sometimes, the luck simply was not there.

None of this was present in Mack Bolan's consciousness at that moment, however. He was a player, not a gambler—and the game was life itself. He did not look to luck but to excellence, and he cultivated that with a dedication to be found only in a life-and-deather.

During the next few moments, this life-and-deather would need every erg of human excellence within his reach.

And, sure, he knew it.

It had been a long and nervous night and chief bodyguard Jack "Sailor" Santini was glad to see it ending. He turned off the outside lighting and stepped onto the front porch for a quick breath of fresh air and a quiet appraisal of the situation out there. The nippy air felt good and the world looked beautiful, too beautiful for the mess the human race was making of it. The ex-fisherman from San Francisco had become something of a nature lover since his arrival in the big sky country a few years back—an appreciation with its seeds, probably, imbedded behind the prison walls where Sailor Jack had left twelve years of his life. He and Tommy Rizzi had been boyhood pals, growing up together in the North Beach district of San Francisco. Rizzi went east at eighteen and made a connection with the New York mob; Santini went down to the sea on his uncle's fishing boats, married the passionate Sylvia, and began an annual harvest of new mouths to be fed—far too many to be handled comfortably from the uncertain proceeds of a fisherman's life.

Santini began taking "side jobs" with the power brokers of underworld San Francisco—mostly muscle work and an occasional "body contract." The powerfully built fisherman quickly established a reputation as a reliable "arm and leg man" and, later, as a "mortician" or "garbage man." His mainline profession contributed nicely to that latter sideline; it was estimated, by the prosecuting attorney who finally nailed him, that Santini had disposed of more than twenty corpses of murder victims during his five years with the fishing boats. It had also been suspected that the sailor himself was directly involved in several of those murders. He'd finally gone down on a conspiracy rap which accounted for his first five years in San Quentin and during which time Sylvia divorced him and took off somewhere with the kids. Santini had never seen any of them again. He did, though, see San Quentin a couple more times over the years.

It was Tom Rizzi who pulled him out of that circle of defeat, bringing him to Denver and at least an air of respectability. Rizzi had struck it big, fronting in the mountain state for an eastern combination of interests and gradually building his own little base of power.

Rizzi had never been a button man. He'd never broken arms or buried bodies and he'd never been convicted of anything beyond a couple of simple misdemeanors. He was a charm guy, a brain specialist—a "natural," as they used to call that type in San Francisco.

Sailor Jack hated Tom Rizzi's guts.

Which was not too surprising. The Sailor hated everybody. A white-collar con at Q had once quoted some philosopher as having said that mankind was God's greatest mistake—and that summed up Sailor Jack Santini's philosophy in a nutshell.

He did not like anybody, himself least of all.

But, yeah, that world out there was beautiful. It overshadowed the mistake that was mankind, played it down, put the garbage in its place.

So philsophized the arm and leg man from San Francisco on that chilly morning in Denver's south side as he faced the new day. He walked to the edge of the porch and lit a cigarette, then called out, "Jim! Eddie!"

A skinny kid appeared from the shadows of the portico, bundled in an overcoat and moving stiffly. "Yeah, Jack."

"Where's Eddie?"

The second one appeared at the south corner and called up, "Right here. What is it?"

"Another day," Santini growled. "You boys tuck it in and go on home. Thanks for standing by."

"Next time, make it a summer night," said the kid at the portico.

"Mr. Rizzi appreciates the help, you know that. You'll see it on your next paycheck. Go on, get outta here, go get laid or something."

The bodyguard watched as the muscle contractors gathered their crews into the vehicles at the curb and quietly departed. It was a hell of an expense for nothing, Santini was thinking. It would be much cheaper to keep a full crew standing, on standard salary arrangements. But Mr. Rizzi the Natural would not go for that. Nothing that obvious. It would hurt the civic-minded image of a legitimate businessman to have a bunch of gunsels standing around in the full light of day. Someone might even get the idea that the natural Mr. Rizzi associated with criminal types, God forbid.

Sailor Jack puffed on his cigarette and watched the vehicles to the street, ruminating darkly on the hypocrisy and natural perversity of the world of men, then he took a last appreciative look at the dawn rays reflecting from the mountain peaks and turned back toward the door.

The gun crews hit the street and turned west. A commotion in the opposite direction froze the Sailor and turned him back around. A hoarse voice had yelled some urgent command; now a guy dressed in a white outfit was sprinting along the street, up there, with a sheriff's deputy hot on his tail. A car roared out of a driveway several hundred feet eastward and gunfire erupted farther east.

Santini muttered, "Oh shit!" and quickly let himself into the house.

Rizzi, Mr. Natural in a silk dressing gown, appeared at the railing of the upstairs foyer to call down: "Jack! I heard gunshots!"

"It's the cops," Santini called back. "Chasing somebody down the street."

"Could it be *him?*"

"Sure. It *could* be Jesus. Also it could be some terrified kid with a hot bag of second-story loot.

Play it careful, though, Tommy. Go back inside and lock your door. Is Al up there?"

"No. He went down to get some coffee."

"Okay. I'll send him up. You stay put."

Mr. Natural nodded curtly and returned to his room. He did not like to be talked to that way, and Santini knew it, but Santini also knew that it was the very thing which made him valuable to a punk like Tommy Rizzi. He'd always ordered the guy around, and the guy had always respected him for it. It had been that way from childhood, even though Tommy had forever been the smarter of the two. Santini did not understand the deeper psychological ramifications of such a relationship but he did recognize that it was there—and he played his cards accordingly.

He was heading for the kitchen to roust the upstairs man when Rizzi's door banged open again, almost like a rebound, and the man in monogrammed silk again appeared at the railing.

This time, he was not alone—and something of the "Natural" look had deserted him.

He was sucking the muzzle of a wicked black pistol and standing there like an immobilized robot, eyes closed, barely breathing, the barrel of that pistol practically buried inside his mouth.

The other guy was big, impressive, cool, in full command. "Don't even blink hard, Sailor," he cautioned in a quiet voice that matched everything else.

Santini had seen sketches of what Mack Bolan was supposed to look like—a mere few hours ago he'd studied the latest batch of police composites—but nothing in those sketches had prepared him for the reality of this guy. It wasn't just the outside looks. There was something that came from inside this guy that you'd never be able to see in a picture, let alone a damn composite sketch. The guy was more than eyes and nose, chin and hairline, ears and cheekbones.

The guy was something more than Jack Santini had ever seen. Reflecting back on that experience, during a more relaxed time, Jack the Sailor would compare Mack Bolan with those ice-peaked mountains out there in the beautiful world. The guy had a stirring effect on the senses.

The vision of that "stirred" Jack Santini into perhaps the first calm of his adult life.

"I'm not blinking, Mr. Bolan," he replied easily, showing the man the innocent positioning of his hands.

"Call Al out here where I can see him."

Santini did so, without cuteness, and further cautioning the youngster: "Don't get heroic, kid. Stay loose, and let's see what the man has in mind."

The kid did precisely that, splashing hot coffee down his leg as he stared into that quiet confrontation, apparently not even aware of the scalding.

"What I have in mind," the man was explaining, "is a short parley with your boss. You get his car and bring it around to the front door. Then you stand there and watch us drive away. Do it cool, and you'll have him back in time for breakfast. Do it dumb, Sailor, and maybe none of us will be around for chow."

"The guy's my meal ticket, Mr. Bolan. I need assurances if I'm going to be cool."

The big guy showed his teeth in a grimace which may have been a smile. "If I'd wanted his head, Sailor, you'd have never known I was here. It's a white-flag meet. You know my reputation."

Sure. The sailor knew all about that.

"Okay. But the kid brings the car around. Uh—the street's full of cops, you know."

Those teeth showed again. "They're chasing east. We'll avoid them." Icily glinting eyes fastened on the kid. "Get the car."

The kid glanced at Santini and hurried outside.

Marvelous, yeah, awesome and beautiful. That guy was something else—and the arm and leg man from 'Frisco was beginning to reassess the place of man in the universe.

They were descending the stairs now. The black auto was now at Rizzi's ear. He was drooling uncontrollably and looking more unnatural with every step. By the time they reached the lower foyer, Bolan was practically holding the punk upright.

Terrified eyes anchored themselves to the cool stare from Santini. "F'God's sake, Jack!" the great man burbled.

"It's okay, Tommy. Be cool, and he won't hurt you."

Sailor Jack moved carefully to the door and outside. The mountains were really dazzling, now, dwarfing and flattening everything but the sky itself and making even that seem accessible to the puny men who stood below it all.

The Sailor and the Kid stood at the front bumper with hands pressed to the cold steel of the engine hood as Mr. Natural and Mr. Awesome got into the car.

A moment later, car and all were gone and the young houseman was marveling, "Did you ever *see* such a guy!"

But Jack the Sailor Santini was looking at the mountains and the big sky. He took his revolver from the shoulder holster and spun the cylinder without looking at it, then put it back away and told the kid: "No. No, I never saw such a guy."

"What d'ya think? Will he let him go?"

Jack Santini was thinking of retirement . . . and a cabin up there at the edge of the big sky.

"Huh?" he responded absently to the youngster's worried query.

"You think Bolan will really let Mr. Rizzi go?"

"Don't tell me you really care," the fisherman growled, and went back up the stairs to nowhere.

7: COMING TOGETHER

The guy was about forty, medium height and slightly built, almost handsome, with closely clipped hair and a pencil-line moustache, dark enough to pass for an Arab, scared enough to be mistaken for an ordinary citizen. He sat stiffly against the passenger door, struggling for self-control, never once looking directly into Bolan's eyes.

The car was a sleek Pontiac with bucket seats, center console. Bolan was at the wheel, cruising slowly through a Littleton residential district.

They'd been underway for ten minutes without a word passing between them. When he thought the tension had built to the breaking point, Bolan pulled to a halt in a deserted shopping center, lit a cigarette, and told his prisoner, "You're in big trouble, Rizzi."

"I know that," the guy muttered. "Can I have one of those?"

Bolan passed him the lighted cigarette and lit another for himself.

"This is your territory—right?"

The mafioso exhaled turbulent gusts of smoke and sighed the reply. "Yeah. Sort of."

"It is or it isn't, guy."

"It is, then."

"So I have you to thank for the little surprise party last night."

"I don't, uh, get you."

"Sure you do. The party in the hills, the costume ball. Everybody came as soldiers."

"Look, I don't know anything about that," Rizzi protested, too much.

Bolan dropped a marksman's medal on the console. The guy winced and hastily averted his gaze from that.

"Too bad," Bolan said coldly. "It was the only value you had to me, guy."

"Wait. Okay. Maybe I do know something. Are you telling me that's my way out?"

"That's what I'm telling you."

"Well, what d'you want?"

"I want Trooper."

The trapped gaze caromed around the interior of the vehicle, finally coming to rest on the death medal. The voice was desperate and resigned at the same time as Rizzi told the Executioner: "Look, you've got me out of my weight. I'm not what you think. All I have here is an office. I'm, uh, a representative. They say do this, I do this—do that, I do that. I've got no weight of my own."

"I don't want your weight, Rizzi. I want Trooper."

"That's what I'm telling you, dammit. I don't even know what you're talking about."

"Too bad," Bolan said coldly. "Okay, Rizzi. Pick up the medal and get out."

The guy's face drained. He mumbled, "What do you . . . ?"

"Get out!"

"Wait! Now wait! I'm trying to be helpful! But you've got to ask sensible questions! I don't know no Trooper!"

Bolan's voice had become glazed with ice. "You knew about the surprise party."

"Yeah. I was told to stay low and stay clear. That's all. I was told to not get involved. Look, we got a big thing going down near the shale fields, a legit thing. They don't want any compromise of that. They want me to keep clean. I had nothing to do with that thing last night."

"But you knew about it."

"Sure, I told you."

"Who told *you*, Rizzi?"

"*They* told me."

"Who are *they?*"

"You know. The men East."

Bolan said, "Uh huh. Tell me again what they said."

"They said it was a dead zone and the thing was on. I was to stay out of it. Completely. Out of it."

"And when did they tell you this?"

"Yesterday. I was having dinner at my club, and I got this call. They said the thing was on. Go home and button up. So I did. I got home a little after seven. And I stayed there all night."

"You've got my interest," Bolan told him. "Keep going."

"Well that's all. I got another call about nine. They said the thing had gone sour. I should stay buttoned up and put out a hard line just to make sure. So we hired some boys for outside security and we sat up all night waiting for further word."

"None came."

"That's right, nothing came. Except you. God's truth, Bolan, that's all I know about it."

Bolan stared at the frightened man for a long moment, then he told him, "Okay, I believe you. What's this thing about the shale fields?"

Those eyes flattened and went dull. "Oh, hey, that's nothing you'd be interested in. It's just a land bang."

"Going into the oil business, Rizzi?"

"No, hell no. That's all government land—I mean, the shale itself is. It's purely a speculation. If they decide to mine those fields, there'll be a boom down there. We're just buying up some real estate, perfectly proper business—a simple speculation in real estate values."

"You have an inside track on the decision to open the fields? Someone in Washington?"

"Aw no, hell no. It's just commonsense. They've got to go after that oil, sooner or later. It's a clean deal, Bolan."

"Uh huh. And you never heard of Trooper."

"God's truth."

"How about Jingo Morelli?"

The guy fidgeted, the eyes returning once more to the death medal then bounding away. "Sure, I know Jingo. Cleveland."

"So what's he doing in Denver?"

"He, uh—hell, I see the guy once or twice a week. He comes in the club. We have a couple of drinks and talk old times. I have nothing in common with that wiseguy. He's a button man, always was, always will be."

"What's he doing in Denver?"

"Goofing off, I think."

"He was at the party last night, God's truth."

"Uh, well, uh . . ."

"All of a sudden I'm not feeling so good about you, Rizzi."

"For God's sake, what do you want me to do? *Hang* myself?"

"That's your decision," Bolan replied icily. "You can fly now and pay later, bub, and that's what I'd recommend. But you'd better decide damned quick."

The guy had gone deathly pale, again. Apparently he'd made his decision—to pay later—and the weight of that decision was doing strange things to him, physically. His hands began to shake and the voice broke as he asked his captor for another cigarette.

Bolan refused the request. "You've had your last cigarette from me, guy," he coldly advised him.

"Okay, look. For God's sake, don't ever quote me on this. Those people are after your ass, and they mean to have it."

"What people?"

"I don't know, for sure. It's something big, I know that. Hush-hush, that kind of thing. Jingo tells me they have a thousand boys holed up around here, just waiting for a whack at you."

"How'd they know I was coming?"

"I don't know that. Well, maybe I do. Jingo said something once about baiting the trap. A soft bait, he called it. Hey—they've been expecting you. Jingo's been around town for more than a month."

"Where does he fit?"

"Who would know? To hear him tell it, he's running the whole damn thing. Which is a bunch of shit, and you know it. Jingo never ran anything in his whole life before."

"But he runs his mouth."

"Yeah."

"What'd he say about these thousand boys?"

"Says they're hot stuff. Hey, you know, come to think—he did mention once—called 'em *attack* teams. I got the feeling he was talking about, uh, you know, *army* guys. *Combat* troops." The guy paled even more noticeably. "Aw hell, Bolan—did you ask?—what was that name? I didn't put it together. Trooper? Did you mean a *guy*, or . . . ?"

It was a convincing show of confusion. Bolan was feeling better about Rizzi, now, but worse about the intelligence pouring from the guy.

"It's a code name, Rizzi," he said coldly. "Put it together."

"Well, hell, I—maybe that's it. Yeah, it has to be. Trooper must be the guy in charge of the troops. Right?"

"You tell me."

"Hell, I don't know. I'm just guessing."

The guy was obviously trying desperately to please Bolan, to make him believe. It was a typical situation, and Bolan recognized it. Once the gag comes off, the rush towards truth is almost like a compulsion to get it all out. And, yeah, Bolan was convinced that the guy was cooperating fully now.

"Put it together," he insisted. "A name dropped, a boast, a swagger—Jingo's good at that. Anything—a name, a title—put it together."

"It's a *captain!*" Rizzi crowed.

"A what?"

"Jingo says he don't take no shit off the 'Captain'! He says the Captain has a broomstick up his ass, but he don't sweep no crap onto Jingo!"

"Captain *who?*"

The excitement faded. For the first time, Rizzi's eyes fell fully onto the cold gaze of the Executioner as he dully told him, "That's all I have, Bolan. I swear, that's all I have."

Bolan believed him. He said, "Pick up the medal and give it to me, Rizzi."

The guy did so, eyes humble, face composed but drooping now into signs of total exhaustion.

Bolan pocketed the medal as he told the lucky man, "Don't forget what it looks like, guy. If I decide to come for you again, only your survivors will see it."

"I appreciate it," Rizzi muttered. "Don't worry. You'll never have to come for me again."

"Keep it together," Bolan suggested, almost smiling.

He opened the door and slid outside.

"Take off and don't look back," he commanded.

The guy said not a word as he struggled across the console and into the driver's seat. As he started the engine, though, he poked his head through the window and said, in a friendly tone, "Take a tip, Bolan, and get out of this state. Get out as quick as you can."

Bolan gave him a solemn wink and watched the vehicle ease away.

The picture was coming together, in Colorado.

And, hell, there was no way out for Mack Bolan.

8: ODDS UP

The streets were coming alive with cops. And the markings on the vehicles revealed the intensity of the hunt. State, county, and city cars were rolling—several cities and more than one county—and those were just the obvious ones. Without a doubt, the word had gone down, and the net had drawn tightly around Denver's southwestern corner.

Bolan had the feeling, also, that more than cops were out there prowling those streets.

He'd gone to ground in a prearranged "drop" near Englewood, on Denver's southern approach. It was a small apartment in a respectable building—one of five which he had carefully selected and rented upon arrival in the area. Each of the widely scattered "retreats" was provisioned for a holding situation—a routine precaution for a man living on the heartbeat, but one which a man like Bolan normally did not expect to actually utilize.

This time, he was thankful for the cautious forethought. The situation here was scary, sure, but it was also intriguing—and he wanted time to unravel the thing before committing himself to a do-or-die bust-out.

He had a hasty meal of scrambled eggs, a quick shower and a change of clothes, then he took his coffee to a pay phone in the lobby of the building to make his scheduled contact with Leo Turrin.

He lit a cigarette and placed the call, then sipped the coffee while counting the rings into that distant connection. The line opened at the proper count and the familiarly gruff voice of his best friend in the world announced, "Yeah, okay, who's there?"

"Hans Brinker," Bolan replied. "And I'm skating right at the edge, buddy. Is it clear?"

"Yeah, it's clear," Turrin replied, relief flooding that voice. "What are you into?"

"About the second level of hell, I'd say. I guess—"

"Listen, you've got to get out of there," Turrin interrupted. He was Bolan's ace worrier. This time it was right up front, with no room for other emotions. "That whole area is wired for instant destruct. I helped set you up, Sarge—God*dammit* I hate that—they used me just like they used everyone else, just oozing the word out and knowing it would find its level. I should've known better, I should've—"

"Hey, hey—cut it out," Bolan said mildly. "What have you got?"

"Sheer hell, that's what I've got. Forget about level two—this time it's the whole joint, horns and all, and it's the slickest operation I ever saw. They've been putting this thing together for months. I'd have never thought it possible, but they've—listen, you've got to cut and run. There's no way you can beat this combination."

"What *is* the combination, Leo?"

"Listen, I've been on the horn with the New York headshed since just after I talked to you. *Their* nickel, not mine. They had me on the grill all this time, making me go over and over again every little thing I could tell them about you. What you eat, *when* you eat, how you part your hair. And, listen, the guy doing the asking is no clown. He—"

"Who was it?"

"I don't know the guy and nobody bothered with introductions. Talks with a sort of a southern drawl, uses military jargon, cusses a lot, has a springtrap mind."

"This was New York?"

"Yeah, the commissioners. Augie came on first and told me to answer the man's questions. Then a couple of guys had a go at me before this cornpone colonel took over. He—"

"Is that a figure of speech or . . . ?"

"Yeah. I got no hint at all of who or what the guy is. But then, after the inquisition, Augie came back on the horn and we chatted for a few minutes. That old man is rubbing his hands in anticipation of your head, friend. He can already feel it. Listen, he let it drop that they've been sucking you toward Colorado for months now. I don't know exactly what the combination is, but Augie is sure rolling high with it. Here's the impression I got. It's a three-layer structure of cops, military, and the mob. The mob is providing the suck, the military is the hard machine, the cops are the containment forces. I don't know how this happened, Sarge, without me getting a whiff of it. I let you down. And I just feel miserable about the whole—"

"It's okay, Leo. Think hard, now, and tell me something. Your call came from New York. You talked to Augie, first. Then he handed you over to these other guys. Can you say for a fact that the other guys were in New York? Or could that have been a three-point conference call?"

Silence ruled the wire for a moment, then Turrin quietly replied, "I assumed that they were there together. But, yeah, I guess it could have been a conference. It was a security line, though—you know, a scrambler. But—well, I don't know. Does it matter?"

"It could, yeah. Did you ever brush up against the intelligence boys while you were Army, Leo?"

"Once or twice, yeah."

"These people, uh . . ."

"Yeah, same image. Went like a de-briefing. Those guys are military, Sarge."

Bolan sighed. "Okay, Leo. Thanks. It fits everything I've touched out here. Any word yet from Hal?"

"He wants you to call him direct. Wouldn't give me a hint. Closed as a clam. He got your package, but he wouldn't even discuss it with me. Says it's a case when the least I know the better off I am."

"That's probably true," Bolan said. "Watch yourself, Leo. I'm afraid we have a whole new ball game. A cozy marriage here could make you an unwanted stepchild, damn quick. Be sure you know who your friends are and move very quietly even around them."

"Yeah, I'm getting that," the undercover cop replied grimly. "When I first talked to Hal, earlier this morning, he swore he knew nothing about this combination. If they've even bypassed him to marry up—well, yeah, it *is* a new game."

"Watch your tracks, Leo."

"Yeah. I'll do that. You get your ass out of those mountains."

"Can't. All I can do now is sit it out."

"You can't do that either, Sarge. Not for long. They didn't suck you in there for a casual romp and a run. They'll wait you out. You know that."

Bolan sighed. "Yeah. Well, I'm playing the ear right now, Leo. Maybe I'll have a better handle after I've talked to Hal."

"Sarge?"

"Yeah. I'm still here."

"Listen. You can't even *fight* these guys. They've got too much going."

"What are you suggesting? A white flag? That's sudden death and you know it. Once I'm in the box—"

"I was thinking maybe a deal, through Hal. A quiet surrender, a super maximum security detention, and then . . ."

"And then what?" Bolan inquired mildly.

"You're right, it wouldn't work," Turrin said dismally. "It'd be a field day for the media, though. You might think of it that way. The boys would get to you, sure, but you'd sure go out with a blaze of attention."

"Thanks," Bolan said drily. "Give my apologies to the press corps, will you, Leo. I'm not going that way."

Turrin tried a chuckle which did not quite make it and he was obviously struggling toward lightness as he asked his old friend, "Hey, you aren't really down to thinking about how you'll go out, are you?"

"I've been down to that since the beginning," Bolan told him soberly. "Nothing's changed, Leo. Except the odds."

"Yeah, well . . ."

"Thanks for worrying, Leo. Save it for yourself, though. Ringing off. I want that talk with Hal."

"Hey, uh—anything you'd like me to tell Johnny?"

The kid brother. What to tell him?

Bolan asked, "Is he happy with his new home?"

"Seems to be. He's got a horse. Well, a colt, anyway. Yeah, he's happy."

"Tell him nothing, Leo."

"Okay, sure. Uh, dammit. I hope—I hope . . ."

"You're a good friend, Leo. Take care."

Bolan hung up, stared at the telephone for a moment, then fed in another dime.

It was time to say goodbye to another old friend.

9: BETS OFF

Brognola stood immobile at the window of his operations room, half of his mind on the clock and the other half on the stack of computer print-outs which was growing steadily.

The entire office staff froze when the "straight line" beeped with an incoming call. The operations chief glanced at Brognola then scooped up the instrument and announced, "Justice Two."

He gave Brognola an eye flash and nodded his head.

"Freeze it," Brognola growled and hurried into his inner sanctum.

He picked up the call in there.

"Striker here," identified the damnedest guy.

"Are you okay?"

"For the moment, yeah. I just talked to Sticker. He reads a three-layer deck. What are you reading?"

"Treason, maybe," Brognola growled. "Either that or the slickest con I've ever encountered. There's nothing official going down here, Striker."

"Then what is it?"

"This is a straight line, you know. I can't say everything that's in my mind, not in this town, not anymore. I can tell you this. The men you sent me do not exist. They died in Vietnam, a long time ago. I'll tell you something else. Your vehicle doesn't exist. It was destroyed at Fort Logan eight months ago."

"Well, well."

"Yeah. Listen, I'm running down some interesting streets right now. It will take another five to six hours to just analyze the data that's pouring from the computer. Are you in a cool drop?"

"Cool, yeah, but getting warmer by the minute. I doubt that I can count on another five or six hours. Things are stacking up out here, and very fast. All I want from you, Hal, is an identification. Friend or foe—what is it?"

"Too early to say for sure," the fed replied. "But if it's friends, they sure carry a peculiar odor. That, uh, government reservation you sent me, Striker—it's for real. It's not Army, though—Department of Interior. Some months back there was a move instigated from somewhere inside the Pentagon to transfer the property to Army. The site has been in an inactive status for years. It was some sort of a scientific research station, something to do with glaciation, watersheds, and so forth. Anyway, Army wanted it and the transfer got started through the paper mill. Then it was bounced back on some routine inquiry and no one could locate the originating office."

"What is that office, Hal?"

"Domestic Programs section—some outfit called Civil Contingency Reaction Force. That was an outfit that existed for about twelve hours—on paper only. I remember it. We knocked it down at NSC. Some sort of wild, counterrevolutionary idea. Anyway, the transfer of the property never went through. It's still carried on Interior's inactive lists."

"Someone's living there, Hal."

"Yeah, well, I'm treading lightly until I get more information. If we find that someone at the Pentagon has shotgunned through an illicit operation, there'll be some heads rolling."

"Meanwhile," Bolan said, sighing, "I have this problem, Hal."

"I suggest that you try to duck it. I have all channels open to Denver, so rely on what I am about to say as true. Someone out there has been very busy organizing an area-wide tactical strike plan. Even has my own people rung in on it—the FBI, federal marshals, parks department—even the treasury boys, I understand. They're calling it a Regional Strike Force, and it is at full alert at this very moment with you-know-who as their target. I don't know how you're going to get out of there, Striker, but I can tell you how you're *not* going to get out. You're *not* going to get out by rail, plane, or bus, and you're not going to get out via highway."

"Who'd you say strung this together?"

"I didn't say, because I don't know. It apparently started at the grass roots, and not even my people on the scene can tell me exactly when or by what magic all those diverse agencies were coaxed into such a beautifully cooperative effort. I'm looking into that, also."

"I'm looking for a Captain somebody," Bolan mused.

"An army captain?"

"It would seem so."

"That civil reaction force was the brainchild of an army captain," Brognola recalled. "It would have made him a major if we'd gone along with it. Hold on a minute." He pushed in the intercom and ordered the CCRF file. "I believe I can give you a name, for what it's worth."

"It could be worth a lot," Bolan assured him.

The operations chief hurried into the office and opened a manila envelope for Brognola's scrutiny. He reported to Bolan, "Harrelson, Franklin P. Line officer, combat infantry. A string of decorations almost as long as yours."

"I know the guy," Bolan replied quietly.

"It means something, then?"

"I don't know, Hal. Yeah, maybe it does. Is Harrelson a southerner?"

"Says here he's a native of Arkansas."

"Uh huh, okay, same guy. You need to talk to Sticker about that."

"I do?"

"You sure do. And dig hard on that busted force. I believe I've found my enemy."

"Wait a minute, now. You're saying . . ."

"I'm saying it's a cosmetic force. Harrelson couldn't sell his army to the NSC so he took it to another market. Look into the computer accesses at the Pentagon, particularly with regard to personnel files and material. Look for a connection to Harrelson, especially with regard to surplused or missing equipment. I'm thinking of Southeast Asia now, Hal, and the final disposition of all that stuff we sent over there. You should pull a computer check, also, of all the personnel who served under Harrelson in the combat theaters—who they are and where they are now. Also—"

"What the hell are you suggesting?" Brognola fumed.

"You know what I'm suggesting," the damned guy replied casually. "I'm looking for a killer force, Hal, and I suggest that's what you'd better be doing, too. It's not a pentagon problem, friend, it's your problem. If these guys are what I think they are, and if they've joined up with the mob—well, yeah, friend, you've got one hell of a problem."

"I'm coming out there."

"That's your decision," Bolan told him. "But you may hit more paydirt right where you are. I'm pulling out the stops, Hal. I'm coming out of the hole."

"Well, wait, dammit. You're taking an awful lot for granted. I think you should—"

"I'm reading my gut, Hal. It's never failed me yet. Uh, I guess I called mainly to say goodbye to a friend. But I'm not saying goodbye yet, friend. Hang in there."

"Hold on! I may have another nugget for you. It fell out of a program scan on your government reservation. A lady who lives in that general area filed a complaint three weeks ago. Said that her brother was roughed up by quote some soldiers unquote while he was on a hike. Lady says they threw him face down in a truck and interrogated him with guns at his head, then let him go. The pentagon PRO filed it and forgot it because, as they said, there was no military presence in the area of the complaint. Maybe, uh, you'd want to talk to that lady."

"I guess not," Bolan decided. "I think I have all I need."

"I talked to the lady an hour ago, by phone," Brognola informed his friend. "She denies it all, now. Said it was all a misunderstanding. Striker, the lady was terrified."

Bolan said, "Okay. I'll try to look into it. Maybe there's an angle there."

Brognola passed him the identity and location of the "terrified lady."

"I understand it's a small winter resort," he added. "A sort of shoestring operation run entirely by Mrs. Sanderson and her brother. Uh, I asked to speak to the brother, and she told me he wasn't available. I pressed her, and she fell apart. I was going to give this to my Denver office for follow-up, but I'll hold off a day or so if you'd like to give it a go."

"Do that," Bolan said. The guy's mind was obviously not centered on the conversation. The voice was noncommital, distant. "Don't come out here, Hal," he said, the voice suddenly brisk again. "And tell your people to stand clear."

"I understand," Brognola said quietly.

"Stay hard," Bolan said, and disconnected.

Brognola blinked his eyes and hung up his instrument.

The operations chief closed the CCRF file and asked his chief, "Is it a go?"

"It's a go," Brognola muttered. "Hit it with everything we've got. Don't play cute games with anyone. If you hit a snag anywhere—I mean *any-*

where—refer the problem directly to my attention."

The guy grinned and hurried back to his station.

Brognola dropped his weight to a corner of the desk, bit the plug out of a cigar, and said aloud to the room at large: "Damn, damn. Here we go again."

10: GOING

The tension in that neighborhood was enough to twang the hairs in Bolan's nose. The police presence was still out there, visible, persistent, on the prowl and making no bones about it. That invisible presence was out there, also, though—and this was the one of greatest concern to the man in the web. The sweep was reminiscent of another time, another place—and Bolan recognized it. "Saturation Baker" they'd called it, in the hellgrounds. They'd used it to sweep liberated villages of hidden enemy presence. The technique had proven quite effective in Vietnam. It was a simple suck plan, designed to flush the hidden enemy into the open, utilizing psychological sleight-of-hand to encourage the enemy to reveal his position. And, yeah, it was a simple game. You simply showed yourself, in great force, and you maintained that visibility while conducting a house-to-house sweep. Sooner or later the enemy would bolt, timing his withdrawal to avoid the visible forces. Meanwhile, you were playing all the withdrawal routes with your invisible force which suddenly became highly visible at the point of contact.

Yeah, Bolan recognized the saturation sweep.

And he recognized the military mind behind it.

Frank Harrelson had developed Saturation Baker to a fine art. It had been his specialty during a war of specialists, and his combat teams had formed the cutting edge of the pacification program. Continued excellence in a combat theater does not go unnoticed—particularly not by the professional soldiers who people that theater. For a man at war, the chief form of recreation is talking—and a lot of soldiers had spent a lot of admiring conversation on the redoubtable Captain Harrelson of Pre-Pac Charlie. The guy had become a legend in a land of legends, as had Bolan himself. It had perhaps been inevitable that the two were thrown together in a number of joint missions—Bolan's team at the point and showing the way, Harrelson's Houdinis swooping in for the big broom and turkeyshoot.

Yeah. Mack Bolan knew the hardass captain with the cornpone drawl. And there was little doubt in his mind, now, that Pre-Pac Charlie had turned its cutting edge into the Get Bolan turkeyshoot. It was not an intellectual judgment but a gut assessment. Something had gone sour for Harrelson, back in 'Nam. For some undisclosed reason, the guy had been rotated to rear area duty in a noncombative role. Campfire gossip built many scenarios into that mystery but no facts. People had reported seeing Harrelson from time to time, however, in hellground situations where he should not have been seen—deepening the mystery and intensifying the talk that Captain Harrelson was "into something new and big."

Whatever that "something" was, it had not materialized in the hellgrounds by the time Bolan quit that place. He had never seen or heard of Harrelson again, until that surprising conversation with Hal Brognola from this latest front porch of hell.

Tied to the disclosure by Leo Turrin regarding his interrogation by a southern-talking military type, it seemed too much and too tight for coincidence.

And, yeah—Bolan knew now what he was up against.

Pre-Pac Charlie. Psychological sleight-of-hand. The show of force, the feint, the big wallop. He'd tasted it, already, on a lonely road leading to the highlands. He'd smelled it, strongly, in a brooding neighborhood in Cherry Hills.

And it was twanging his hairs in this apartment complex at the edge of hell.

Point and counterpoint.

There was but one way to play the game. Bolan returned to his apartment and again changed clothes, this time selecting a conservative business suit, white shirt, subdued tie. He retained the Beretta, in shoulder harness, but added a "show piece"—a .38 snub nose chief's special clipped to the belt at hip level. Then he selected a snapbrim hat and went down to join the search for a fugitive.

He timed his exit from the building to coincide with the cruising approach of a police vehicle, which immediately pulled to the curb and halted as he ran up the street to meet it.

"I'm Joe Carson, CSP," he told the startled patrolman. "Think I've found our man. Let's get some help."

The guy had the mike to his mouth and was sending the word when Bolan slid into the vehicle, beside him. The patrolman was young, probably a green kid, and Bolan hated to do it to the guy, but he had to play them as he found them. "Second floor, front," he added to the report. "There's a rear exit and roof access."

The young cop nodded with understanding and passed that info along, also. True to Bolan's expectations, the report was going down on a tactical net, not to the regular police dispatcher—and Bolan knew who, beside the police, would be monitoring that net.

The invisible ones, that's who.

He meant to make them visible . . . and he did.

A cleaners truck lurched around the corner at the next intersection north and immediately nosed into the curb. To the rear, a bread truck hove into view and took up the holding position south.

The young cop at Bolan's left hand told him, "They're ringing it in"—an explanation of the coded commands issuing from the police radio. "Did you actually see the guy?"

Bolan replied, "Yeah, I think so."

The police would not be the only ones "ringing it in." The Houdinis would be moving in force, also, responding to that alert and taking up positions along every possible escape route.

"Take me to the corner stake-out," Bolan requested.

"Which one is that?"

"See the cleaning truck?"

"That's it? Okay." The cop put the car in gear and eased into the traffic flow. "Say your name is Carson?"

Bolan nodded. "Stay with your vehicle. Drop me at the corner and circle back. Take position where you were, and don't make a move until the cavalry arrives."

"You think I'm stupid or something?" the youngster inquired, rolling his eyes to emphasize the response.

Bolan stepped out of the vehicle, then leaned back inside to say, "Thanks. Play it close, now."

The kid replied, "Yes, *sir*," and went on.

The uniformed driver of the cleaning truck had noted the arrival, giving him a quick shift of the eyes and then ignoring him.

Bolan crossed over through the light traffic flow, walked around the rear of the vehicle, opened the loading door at the side, and stepped in. A couple of dresses and a pair of slacks hung from an overhead rack, in plastic bags. A portable radio and a shotgun lay there just inside the door. The guy at the wheel was scowling back at him with a mixture of puzzlement and apprehension.

Bolan said, "It's paydirt, soldier. You can look happier than that."

The guy broke into a grin. "Hell, I thought you were a cop," he replied.

"Come back here," Bolan commanded. "Let's check our signals."

"No time, sir. The cops are wheeling. As slick as our bird is, you know he's not going to just sit there and let them come. He's probably already looking for a path through that circle of steel."

"Are *we* set?"

"Yes, sir. All units are on the line."

The guy was a forward scout, nothing more. In the game plan which Bolan understood so well, his job was to watch and report movements. The main force would take care of the actual contact work, at a time and place of their choosing.

"Is the chopper in the air?" Bolan inquired casually.

"Yes, sir. I just heard them reporting in over Red Rocks, heading this way."

The cincher, sure. They wouldn't try it again without the chopper.

The police were moving in cautiously, sealing off the street, deploying fire teams, invading the buildings to either side of the target building. The whole thing was moving very smoothly—and almost entirely to Bolan's own timetable.

He told the Houdini, "Watch it closely," and returned to the sidewalk. A moment later he was around the corner and moving purposefully along the side street—and one block east, he encountered the second scout line.

There were two of them, seated stiffly in a late model Ford sedan. They were not the law and they were not the mob. For all their civilian look, they were military scouts, and Bolan wasted neither time nor words on these two. He wanted their vehicle, with its radio and possible other intelligence. He leaned in with the silent Beretta and gave each a quick pop between the eyes before either could react to the situation or even assess it.

War, yeah, was hell—but Bolan hadn't invented the game and it was not possible, at this stage, to write in special accommodations for the self-invited intruders into this very private war. Mercenaries—they'd become the worst kind of enemy.

The hi-shock Parabellums took them quick if not so clean. Bolan dumped the bodies into the street and took charge of the vehicle, swinging about in a sedate U-turn and continuing eastward in a methodical withdrawal.

The alarm went down almost immediately, the radio in the captured car squawking: "Scout Five is off station! Scout Five! Report!" And, a moment later: "It's a flush! He's rolling east in Scout Five! All units—belay that, belay it. Possible diversion. Primary units remain on station! Secondary units will close on Scout Five! Communications Plan Two!"

That channel immediately went dead and there was no time for Bolan to search for the "Plan Two" channel. Two units were already upon him—one coming up strong on his rear, another fishtailing into the intersection just ahead and trying to block the escape route. The smallest delay, now, would be catastrophic. He tromped the accelerator and swung the wheel, careening around that imperfect plug with two wheels on the sidewalk at the same instant that the four occupants of the plug vehicle were scrambling clear of what must have seemed an inevitable collision.

Unfortunately, for them, two of the scramblers found themselves in the wrong place and time. Bolan's plunging vehicle caught them squarely in mid stride, sending one hurtling off into the brick wall of a building and the other rolling across the street in the opposite direction.

Fortunately, for Bolan, the other two were too caught up in the scramble for survival to have time or inclination for any sort of offensive action.

He was through and powering into the turn at the intersection when the tail car tried the same maneuver without finding the same degree of success. It was a lighter vehicle and did not fare quite so well at the curb. The driver lost control at that point and the vehicle momentarily wallowed then kneeled left and plunged off in an arcing path toward the plug car then tilted onto its side and completed the final few yards in a grinding slide to eternity.

Bolan heard the impact of the collision and experienced the flash in his mirror as spilled gasoline ignited and whoofed into a towering explosion. He could not have played it better if that had been his intent—which, of course, it was not—and he was not a guy to take lightly a special favor from the universe.

That hellish chaos back there would very probably be enough to spring him from the closing jaws of Saturation Baker.

He was betting on it, anyway, and setting his sights for the high country. He was not retreating now, but searching for an angle of attack.

A "terrified lady" who operated a small winter resort in the very lap of the enemy stronghold just could be the one to provide that angle.

Bolan meant to find out.

Even if, in the end, the universe picked up *all* the marbles.

11: WINTER HEAT

He stuck to secondary roads and navigated by the gut, often driving five miles to realize one true mile toward his goal, avoiding the obvious danger points and ever mindful of the unusual activity in the air overhead. At one point he spotted three helicopters converging in a systematic search pattern at low level while a spotter plane circled high above them.

It was at this point that Bolan took brief sanctuary in a thick stand of trees and undertook an examination of the captured enemy vehicle. It was actually a command vehicle, this fact evidenced by the ultra-sophisticated communications gear which it carried—a powerful set combining UHF and VHF capabilities with pushbutton channel selection. He found sectored topographical maps and communication codes, recognition signals, utilization plans, and various other items of useful intelligence. There was also a "familiarization packet"—physical description and composite sketches of Bolan, a rather detailed biography and a resumé of his war through the campaign in Canada coupled with an "M.O. Profile."

The whole thing bespoke a determined effort by professionals who knew precisely what they were doing and how to do it. They apparently had the resources, also, to make it work. Bolan's job would be to make it work against them, if that were possible.

The radio proved to be a big step in that direction. The enemy knew, of course, that Bolan had possession of one of their command cars and therefore full communications access. There was no way, however, that they could change their communications gameplan short of a complete refitting of all their vehicles. Obviously they could not do this at such a critical point. They could only play the game they had, with all possible pressure, hoping to force their quarry to abandon the vehicle or—at the least—keep him too busy to discover its secrets. That failing, they could only pursue to their best ability and hope for the best. Obviously they were doing so.

Bolan found their air search on a UHF channel and the ground game on VHF. He waited until the air search began moving east and south then resumed his northwesterly advance, carefully picking his way past the picket lines on the ground. The morning was all but gone, the air again crisply thin, and the radio signals a faint blur in the background of his consciousness when he emerged high above it all, on Highway 72, and made a quick run into his base camp near Peaceful Valley.

The campground was nearly deserted when Bolan pulled in behind the warwagon. Two trailers and a pickup-camper were all that remained, and these seemed to be preparing for departure. He was covering the captured car with a tarp and casually studying the two long-haired men in the pickup as it slowly drew abreast of his campsite.

The pickup halted beside him as the youth behind the wheel lowered his window, smiled, and said, "Peace."

"Let's hope so," Bolan replied, smiling back.

"You must've come in late. That's a nice camper you got there."

"Thanks," Bolan said. "Yeah, it's pretty nice."

"Did you get the flash?"

"The what?"

"The weather warning. Winter storm coming. They say it dropped two feet of wet snow last night over in Utah. Coming this way, man."

Bolan glanced at the sky. "Guess it's about that time, isn't it," he commented.

"Never know, in these parts," the longhair replied amiably. "Uh, I noticed your license plate. In case you don't know, it can get pretty mean up here in a snowstorm. You could get isolated for days."

"Thanks," Bolan said. "I'm pulling out."

"You got some kind of ground on that camper—know that? I came over awhile ago to tell you about the storm. I just touched the damn thing and got a shock."

"Sorry. I'll check it out."

The kid smiled and sent the pickup on its way.

Bolan knew all about that "ground," thanks. It

was part of the warwagon's security system—not hot enough to harm even a small child but enough to discourage casual snoopers. Certain critical points would impart a charge sufficient to dishearten the most determined break-in attempts. He deactivated the system and transferred the useful contents of the car to the warwagon, then secured the tarp and installed a towbar. The remaining two campers had departed when he completed the hook-up, leaving him in much-desired seclusion and affording the opportunity for a much-needed camouflage job. He put a new license plate on the Ford, matching the Louisiana plates being displayed on the van, then removed the wheel covers and sailed them into the woods.

Next, he went to work on the van's reversible side panels, altering the color scheme and completing the transformation with magnetic decals suggestive of the huntsman who had been everywhere and bagged everything.

The total job required less than twenty minutes, and while there was no way of completely submerging such a vehicle, the new look would at least partially confuse identification in an area where campers of every description were in profusion.

Bolan was satisfied with the new look.

He went inside and prepared a quick meal while programming his own communications capability to match the enemy's, then he went aft with the food and unconsciously devoured it while integrating the new intelligence info into the master data bank. This completed, he punched into the mobile telephone network and triggered a "collection" from an automated answering service in Kansas City. Two coded contacts were in that collection—one from Leo Turrin, timed in at ten o'clock that morning, another from an unidentified source in Las Vegas.

He returned Leo's call first, running through the elaborate sequence required to get the guy on a no-danger line, and the big-little man from Pittsfield was all in a lather when the contact finally jelled.

"Listen, I've been busy as hell all morning. What's your present situation?"

"High and dry, for the moment," Bolan assured him. "What do you have, Leo?"

"I can't believe what I have, Sarge. I'm still trying to sift it out. No facts now—I don't have any facts—Hal won't even talk to me and the old men in New York have gone into deep freeze. But, Sarge, take off the cuffs. They're trying to suck you, pure and simple. Scratch what I said about military input. It's purely a mob operation. The military part is just a disguise. They're the same kind of military that you are. But, hell, they've got—they've got . . ."

"I know, Leo," Bolan said. "Don't worry about it. I'm onto them. What I'd like from you is—"

"Sarge, wait a minute! Hear me out, first. Listen, this is something really big. Much bigger than it looks on the surface. The way it comes together from the odors I've been getting this morning, this move on you is nothing but a proof mission."

"What does that mean?"

"A warmup. Look, the ice is broken now. People close to the old men are starting to sigh and grin. They're nodding their heads and saying yeah, yeah—if we can do this to Bolan then we can do it to the other guy."

"*What* other guy, Leo?"

"There's the deep freeze, Sarge. I just don't know. But it's something damned big, you can believe that. And listen, when did you last talk to Hal?"

"Then you don't know the other side, either. Hal won't talk to me, but I have my sources down there in never-never land. Hal is onto something, and that whole town could blow sky high if he's tracking true."

"What's he tracking?"

"Something to make the past disturbances in that town insignificant in the comparison. I have only the rumbles, Sarge, but it's something to do with the Pentagon and a big-shot general who, it seems, is in the mob's pocket."

Bolan lit a cigarette and blew the smoke into the transmitter.

"Sarge?"

"Yeah, I'm here. When you put it all together, Leo, what do you have?"

"Hell, I don't know. I just don't know. But it makes me sick at my stomach, Sarge. You know? My gut has put it together but it hasn't yet reached my head. And listen, just before I took this walk, the word came down that they were laying all over you in Denver, had you pinned down and unable to move. True?"

Bolan chuckled drily. "Not true, Leo. I'm glad they think so, though."

The little guy laughed nervously as he replied, "Well, okay, I'm happy to hear the other side of that. Uh, I guess that's all I have for now. Why don't we meet here again in exactly two hours."

Bolan punched a timer on his console. "Okay. That's a date. Thanks, Leo."

"You're going to have to stop that movement out there, you know. We can't rely on Hal and the smothered bureaucrats. If this thing really materializes into a head-rolling scandal—well, there are heads and there are heads. Hal's could be the one to roll."

"Yeah," Bolan replied quietly.

"So it's your baby, start to finish."

"A few hours ago," Bolan observed, "you were yelling at me to cut and run."

"That was a few hours ago. This is now. You have to take them out, Sarge. If you don't, God only knows what their next round will be."

"You feel that strongly about it?"

"I do. Say the word and I'll join you. I can get a flight in thirty minutes—be out there by sundown, your time."

Bolan pondered the offer for a brief moment before replying, "Thanks, Leo, no. I'd rather have you where you are. Keep digging, huh?"

"Will do. Stay hard, man."

"You know it," Bolan said, and rung off.

He thoughtfully smoked the cigarette down to his fingers then put it out and made the Las Vegas call.

A perky female voice responded to the first ring. "Able Group."

"Give me another number," Bolan told it, without preamble.

She did so, in that same perky tone, then added, "Give it a minute."

He killed the connection, waited a minute, then made the call to that "other number," a pay phone, he hoped.

It was. She said, "Mack, oh honey, it's so good

to hear your voice. It's okay, I'm in a phone booth on Fremont Street."

It was Toni Blancanales, the Pol's kid sister—now an equal partner with Death Squad survivors Schwarz and Blancanales in an electronic detection agency called Able Group.

Bolan was grinning as he told her, "Great to hear yours, too, Toni. I'm in the light, though, so let's make it short and sweet."

"Short, fine," she replied with a wry twist to her words, "sweet, I don't know so much. Do you know a man by the name of Harrelson?"

Bolan's grin vanished. He replied, "Maybe. Why?"

"The word is out, urgent and pleading, that he wants a meet with you. It's supposed to be life or death—yours."

"How did you get that word, Toni?"

"The jungle telegraph. He's been contacting all the old troops, I take it, and asking everyone to pass the word along."

"Okay. What is that word?"

"He's at Winter Park, Colorado. A ski lodge there, called Snow Trails."

"That's it?"

"That's it," she said, sighing. "Gadgets said I shouldn't tell you, but—I can't make a decision like that."

"You did right, Toni," he assured her. "What's happening in Vegas?"

He could picture her wrinkling that pert nose as she replied, "Same old stuff. We're de-bugging a casino for a paranoid client who sees a badge behind every lapel."

Bolan chuckled and said, "Give the guys my love."

"*All* of it?"

"All you can't handle," he said soberly.

"Well they're not going to get a drop," she told him, just as soberly. "Uh, are you anywhere near Colorado?"

"I'm afraid so, Toni."

"Oh. Well, dammit. Be careful, huh?"

"Name of the game," he assured her.

"Do we, uh, have to go on like this? Meeting in secret? Can't we, uh, get together over a cold night and, uh . . . ?"

Bolan was chuckling as he told her, "All I can see from here is heat. When I find a cold night, though . . ."

"It'll never happen," she sniffed, and hung up.

She was, Bolan knew, probably right about that.

There was nothing ahead for Mack Bolan but heat. And, yeah, he had to go out and meet it.

12: THE OTHER

He crossed the Divide at Rollins Pass, making the approach to Winter Park via the back road, and immediately ran into heavy snowfall. The journey of less than twenty air miles had consumed several hours of ground travel in light snow along the east slope. The west slope had obviously been under heavy snow conditions for most of that time. A ranger had stopped him just west of the pass and suggested that he turn around at that point and return to East Portal.

"Is the road still open?" Bolan wanted to know.

"For now, yes sir," the ranger told him. "But I can't guarantee you'll make it through. Especially with that tow vehicle."

The situation was looking pretty grim, all right. Several inches of snow had accumulated already. Visibility was down to about a hundred feet and, as the ranger pointed out, "It's a major storm system. Things are going to get much worse."

But Bolan was less than five miles from his goal. He told the ranger, "I believe this cruiser can bull on through."

The guy shook his head disgustedly at that decision but helped Bolan install tire chains, then sent him on his way with the parting advice: "If you get stalled, stay with your vehicle."

Bolan thanked the man and went on, activating the optic and navigational support systems, which helped a little but not enough, and very quickly he found himself questioning the wisdom of his decision.

He was in a world apart, a frozen world of white stillness and vertigo-producing closeness, total isolation, constant danger.

He chuckled self-consciously at his own sudden uneasiness.

So what was new?

The snow, the whiteness, that was all that was new. It was not a different world but merely a different-colored one. The snow was not his enemy. It could, he knew, be his dearest friend in the challenging hours ahead.

So . . . who *was* the enemy?

Bolan had learned to trust Leo Turrin's guts almost as much as his own. What was the "big thing" that was producing all the smiles and nods in the New York headshed? Who was the "other guy" whom they hoped to hit, after Bolan?

Why had Harrelson sent the message, and what did the message really mean? Was it a challenge, a suck, or a genuinely concerned attempt to reach an old friend with a dire warning?

They *had* been friends, sort of, at one time.

You didn't have to exactly *approve* of a guy in order to like him. And Bolan had liked the guy. He'd been a cool warrior, nervy and daring but also very methodical—a sure hand to take in partnership with life hanging on every heartbeat.

What sort of hand was Frank Harrelson now extending to Mack Bolan?

It had not been difficult for Bolan to accept the idea that Harrelson was his principal enemy of the moment, not at all difficult. And his immediate reaction to Toni's message had been entirely natural: Harrelson could not know that Bolan had linked him to the Colorado turkeyshoot; this was merely another suck, designed to lure the prey into the web. The "jungle telegraph" was not all that swift a means of communications. That word could have gone down days ago, and probably had—long before the formal hostilities had commenced in this area.

Still, there was an element of uncertainty in the entire hypothesis. Harrelson's "link" to the Colorado action was an entirely circumstantial one.

It was that element of uncertainty which was now propelling Mack Bolan along a hazardous mountain road in a growing snowstorm to a ski lodge near Winter Park. That telephone conversation with Toni Blancanales was not the first time that day when *Snow Trails* lodge entered the picture. Brognola had introduced the place first, as the home and business of a terrified lady named Sanderson.

And, yeah, Bolan's world was growing smaller all the time.

As small and as tight as that zone of visibility in a thickening snowstorm, as threatening and as deadly as that soft and silent fall of intricately patterned crystals of immobilizing stuff from above, as uncertain and mysterious as these brooding mountains in a sudden winter storm.

Bolan's world, sure. But it was the only one he had. And he had to make it work for himself.

The resort was well marked and not at all difficult to find, despite the weather conditions. Far more difficult was the task of laying out the place, getting its lie and physical plant. It seemed to consist of a central building in the style of a large double A-frame, with small cabins sprinkled about in a random arrangement—the whole thing snuggled onto a small plateau overlooking the ski slopes. Visibility was bad and worsening by the moment, however, and Bolan could not be certain of his perspective.

He had left his vehicles far to the rear, taking the final quarter-mile on foot, and the going had been rough. Clad in "life suit" and hooded parka, glare-reducing goggles, heavy boots, he was comfortable enough but would gladly have given someone a thousand dollars for a pair of snowshoes. A foot or more of fresh snow was underfoot, and although there was no wind to speak of, the snowfall was almost as dense as a stationary cloud and the visiblity was nowhere.

He actually felt his way around that property, in a blind reconnaissance which was almost surrealistic as a final picture. He did satisfy himself, however, that the only evident signs of habitation were in that central building. Lights were on in there, and the good-smelling smoke from a wood fire was coming from the chimney. Once he thought he saw the shadow of someone standing at an upstairs window, and as he drew closer, he could hear the sound of recorded music.

There was no disturbance of the snowbed surrounding the house, no tracks, nor were there any signs that the place was anything other than the resort it was supposed to be, all but deserted in the first snow of the season.

An A-frame building is a curious structure, with sloping roofs forming the side walls, windowless except at front and back—a favored design in deep snow country, where the weight of accumulated snow on flat rooftops has been known to collapse conventional structures. This particular design employed two "A" sections in a T arrangement. Bolan had been inside similar buildings, and he could picture in his mind a typical interior layout. A vaulted main living area, chapellike in its soaring height, a small balcony leading to upstairs bedrooms at the rear. In this one, probably the entire upper level of the horizontal "A" section was given to bedrooms, the perpendicular "A" open all the way to the peak of the roof—some forty feet from floor to ceiling. Around to the rear, main level, kitchen and dining room—perhaps another bedroom or two tucked into the eaves where headroom was minimal.

And there was but one entrance at ground level.

It could be a tough one to crack, if cracking it needed. And it probably did. One does not simply saunter up to the spider's parlor, knock on the door, and request entry.

Bolan circled the building several times, certain that he was invisible to any occupants, studying the possibilities and formulating a plan of entry. But when he finally made his move, it was the only move possible.

He went to the front porch and knocked on the door.

Through the glass front, he could see flames dancing from logs in the fireplace. A lovely blonde woman sat in front of it on a white furry rug, knees drawn up and arms encircling them, staring into the flames. She wore blue jeans and a ski sweater, and she seemed totally preoccupied with the contents of her mind, giving no indication of having heard the knock at the door.

Someone else did, though.

He was a guy of about twenty-five, square-jawed and hard, hostile and suspicious. He yelled through the door, "What do you want?"

"I'm in trouble," Bolan yelled back. "Do you have a phone?"

"No phone. You're on private property. Get off."

Bolan raised his goggles, and the two glared at each other through the glass of the door. "You crazy?" Bolan yelled. "A man could die out here! Do you open the door or do I kick it down?"

The guy opened the door, but just a little, and the snout of a Colt .45 appeared there. "You want to kick this down, too?" sneered the man behind it.

Yeah, Bolan did want to do that.

He hit the door with both feet, putting all his weight into it and twisting aside in the backward fall. The Colt roared once and fell to the outside, the shot going wild, the guy going down in a pole-axed drop beyond the rebounding door.

Bolan scooped up the fallen weapon as he rolled

on through, but there was no fight left in the nasty one. He'd obviously taken the full jolt with his forehead; he was unconscious and the head was already ballooning out above the eyebrows.

The blonde lady had come to her feet and covered half the distance to the doorway. She saw the pistol in Bolan's hand, checked her forward motion, and cried out, "There's another upstairs!"

But the warning was unnecessary.

The second man had already charged onto the balcony at the rear, clad in longjohns only and brandishing a long-barreled revolver. His reaction to that situation below him was professional and quick, throwing himself into a sideways dive and tossing off a shot that gouged the wood at Bolan's feet.

The retort from the .45 was, however, quicker and a bit more professional. Three scorching rounds in rapid fire searched through the flimsy decorative wood enclosing that balcony and found target on the other side. The guy's life bubbled away in mid-screech, and the lady turned from that with bugging eyes.

She was a real beauty, a Nordic type with long and graceful lines, and just a charming trace of Scandinavian in her speech. "Are you a policeman?" she gasped.

Bolan replied, "I'm afraid not."

Yeah, a real beauty, even in heart-stopping terror.

"You must run! Quickly! Get help! They are waiting for the president!"

Bolan blinked his eyes at that, and said, "Give me that again?"

"There are more! All around—everywhere—

hundreds! Quickly, please, get away and tell the police!" She was running out of voice. "The president—this weekend—skiing! Please! Please!"

Bolan pushed the door shut, deposited the .45 on a table, and opened the parka to check his own weapons.

Okay.

So now he knew.

He knew why the incredible effort, the fantastic investment, the unbelievable intrigue.

The "other guy" was the President of the United States.

13: TIME IN

Time was always such a relative thing. Ten seconds with your hand pressed to a hot stove could seem like ten minutes. Ten minutes with your arms enfolding the woman you love could seem like ten seconds. In the space of a single heartbeat, a dying man could reexperience his entire lifetime.

Time out of frame, yeah, could screw a guy up.

Bolan was screwed up, right now, and he knew it. It did not particularly help that he knew. He felt like a man living on sixty second time in a world that had suddenly slowed to ten second time—like living in a world where everything but yourself is moving in slow motion.

It seemed that there was a plot to hit the president—up here, yeah, in these mountains. And time had expanded, recalling and rearranging all the events of the past twenty-four hours into a melange of faces, conversations, actions—including the present moment—like a giant jigsaw puzzle whose pieces are dumped onto the floor, and the floor itself is part of the puzzle. It was all there, all of it, and somehow you knew that you had the picture spread before you—yet the picture was not yet put together.

The beautiful lady continued pleading with him to run for it and time in mind continued to slip and spin as he moved eerily through the frozen world, gripped by the certainty of truth in his gut and sinking despair in his heart.

The telephone was smashed beyond repair. The nearest communications point was the warwagon, a quarter-mile to the rear with a winter storm and God knew what else standing across the path. The lady kept insisting that "the others" were out there, somewhere, close enough to have heard the brief firefight. A dead man's blood was dripping from the balcony, a dying man lay at his feet, and a Nordic goddess was babbling an hysterical tale of death to the chief.

Time was out of sync, yeah.

Bolan removed his parka and began unbuckling the combat rig which had been worn beneath it. He took off grenade clusters, munitions belts, weapons belts, utility pouches—arranged them carefully for reassembly—and again pulled on the parka then began the rearming process.

The sight of all that weaponry had an immediate settling effect on the lady. Calm blue eyes watched the preparations for combat as Bolan told her, "Get into something warm, Mrs. Sanderson. We're leaving."

"They are holding my brother," she replied calmly. "They will kill him if I leave."

"They'll kill you both if you don't," he assured her. "Where are they holding him?"

"In the lift house, I believe. At the beginners' slope."

"Okay, we'll get him. Get dressed."

Those eyes flashed and sparkled as she made the decision, whirling toward an open closet near the door and snatching a ski suit.

"You know—my name," she puffed, moving almost frantically again now, as she struggled into the outfit.

It was no time for explanations. He replied, "Yeah," and began stringing the grenades.

"I know yours, too. You're Mack Bolan, aren't you."

He did not confirm the identification, but asked her, "How far away is the lift house?"

"Three hundred meters perhaps."

Nordic, yeah. He wondered fleetingly about the twists of life that had brought this lovely young woman to this place and time. Even more important, though, what would take her the thousand feet to her brother's captors, and the quarter-mile beyond that in a blinding storm to temporal safety, and where would this journey end?

Gruffly, he asked her, "Where's your husband?"

"I am a widow," she informed him, almost absently, as she fumbled with the zipper to the ski togs.

Bolan positioned the AutoMag at his right hip, made a test draw and checked the action. "Where'd you hear my name?"

She replied, without raising eyes to him, "I have heard little else since early this morning. They were expecting you here, earlier. With much excitement and quivering anticipation.

Then, shortly before noon, the helicopter returned with the news that you were being hunted down, in Denver." Her gaze moved to the man on the floor. "Mr. Smith was greatly disappointed with the news. He sulked the afternoon away and became inconsolable when the snow began deepening." The cool gaze found Bolan's. "He wanted to be the one to kill you."

Yeah, time out of sync.

It seemed that he'd known this lady for a long while. He'd first placed eyes on her about ninety seconds ago, yet in that time-frozen melange of overlapping events, they'd been together from the beginning.

He dropped a death medal on "Mr. Smith" and told the lady, "We're out of time. Let's go."

"My name is Giselda. Lars—my husband—called my Undy. You may call me Undy."

"Undy?"

"Yes." Her gaze wavered. "It is short for Undurridis. Do you know her?" She saw the answer in his eyes, and continued: "In Norse mythology, the ski goddess. Not that I—it is an easier name than Giselda."

"Let's hope the name fits," Bolan gruffed. "Who's the ski God?"

"Skade," she replied.

"Call me that, then, and hope it fits, also. Do you have some cross-country skis around here?"

"In the outfit shop," she told him. "Near the lift house."

Bolan was certainly no *Skade*—but he had taken a military ski course in Germany, years ago, and he did know the shovel from the tail. He had, in fact, excelled in cross-country racing and had done a bit of ski mountaineering on a furlough in the Alps. All that had been a while ago, though—and certainly this was no time for a refresher course.

They were moving toward the door when Bolan tensed and lifted his head to an unfamiliar sound, outside, distant.

"It is the snowmobiles!" the woman cried. "They have returned!"

*Snow*mobiles!

He pivoted and dragged the woman with him toward the rear. "How many?" he snarled.

"Five, six! Perhaps more!"

Okay, then. Two men to a buggy translated to too damn many to face squarely, with a noncombatant in tow.

He moved her into the horizontal "A" section and onto an open deck overlooking the rear from a height of about twenty feet. From a hanging drop, then, say ten to twelve feet into cushioning snow.

"Are you game?" he asked her.

She jerked her head in an affirmative nod. Bolan led the way, showing her how, and they dropped together.

To hell with manual skis. Mack Bolan intended to get himself some motorized ones.

Then maybe he and his ski goddess could make like snow birds and fly, fly away. It was a whole new game, now—and the name of it was *disengagement*. He had to make it back to the warwagon and send word to keep the president in Washington.

The "warmup" was over, and the main event was coming up. The president was a ski enthusiast and, sure, back in that melange of time out of sync Bolan could see the announcement of some weeks earlier that the guy would be in Colorado at first snow, to officially open the new ski season.

But why the president? What the hell did anyone hope to accomplish by knocking the guy off?

Those were questions which would have to find their own time. For now, the task was to break clear and get the alarm going down.

He pushed the ski goddess face down into the snow and commanded her to remain there, then began his move—circling out to the rear and doubling back in an arcing approach to the dead zone.

And time was still out of sync. Barely two minutes had elapsed since he'd entered the house. The visibility was holding at about twenty feet, but that was about the only condition that had not changed radically. A wind was coming up, now, and driving the falling flakes in a slanting drop. A barrage of sound was coming with the slant, hot little internal combustion engines, in numbers and in steady approach.

Bolan had to rely entirely upon audibles to feel the moment. Six sounded right, yeah—about six, coming in like the spokes of a wheel toward its hub, moving cautiously in the near-zero visibility conditions, converging on the house. At about fifty feet out, someone out there fired a shot from a handgun. Then, silence descended as all engines sputtered out. A strong voice came down on the wind: "One and Six, hold present position. Two and Five, form a bracket at the rear. Four, back me up. I'm going inside."

"Watch it, Charley," a worried voice called back. "Sammy counted five shots. Could mean anything."

Bolan was moving in on them, placing his feet

carefully while moving with all possible speed in the treacherous underfooting.

A voice very closeby was chuckling with some private joke. Another said, "Cut that. What's the hell's to laugh about?"

"Maybe," replied the chuckler, "Miss Hardass got the drop on Terrible Tom and gave 'im what he's got coming."

"Shut up," said the other, disgustedly.

Four engines roared to life and the approach resumed. One was coming straight toward Bolan. He held his position and lifted Big Thunder—the .44 AutoMag—into the confrontation.

The snow buggy came from nowhere, materializing suddenly as a dark bulk from somewhere beyond space and time—and Bolan had been mistaken about the visibility factor. It was no more than ten feet out and moving cautiously forward, straight at him. Bolan was all in white and no doubt invisible at anything more than armlength distance. The two men in that open vehicle very likely died without knowing that they did so, the big silver hawgleg thundering its two-word greeting in such rapid sequence as to blur into a single report. Both men were practically decapitated by the big mushroom bullets, even though Bolan had targeted entirely by zone trajectory. Time out of sync, sure. He had not seen them until they were dead and tumbling from the vehicle. The engine lugged out and died at Bolan's side. He climbed in and ran his hands along the controls, feeling for an understanding and quickly coming to it. It was like a motorcycle, with handlebar controls.

Meanwhile, all other vehicles had come to a halt, engines again shutting down. A guy near the house shouted, "Who fired? Horse?"

"Not me," came the reply, from nearby.

"Who fired? Dammit! Let's have a roll call!"

Distant voices were shouting numbers at each other as Bolan found the final secret and started the engine. He moved out immediately, traveling recklessly and navigating entirely by instinct in what he hoped was a backtrack along his own path. The sound of his own engine was drowning out all other sounds about him. He had no audible input from the enemy force, but he did sense their concerned movements. Then the house loomed up in his forward vision. He sailed on around to the rear, collected his passenger, and headed for open spaces.

She clung to his arm and cried, "Marvelous, marvelous!"

But Bolan was not so certain of that. For all he knew, they could be heading straight toward a free jump down the mountainside.

The events of the past twenty-four hours had finally caught up with him, collected in his wearied bones, and were now trying to crush him. That vertigo sensation, experienced briefly at Rollins Pass, had returned.

He halted the little ski buggy and told the goddess of skis: "You take it. Let's find that lift house."

"We should be very close," she told him, moving into place as Bolan vacated the control seat.

Very close, yeah. And it hadn't been vertigo. As he stepped down onto the snow beside the vehicle, he found himself poised at the very brink of a steep downhill slope.

All instinctive systems were A-OK. It had, of course, been a damn quick 300 meter run. But that's the way it was, sometimes, with gods and goddesses of the ski—and with time out of frame.

"Stay put," he told the lady. "And don't make a sound. I'll find your brother."

He hoped he would. At that moment he could not have found his own feet had they not been attached to him. And the sounds were swirling about that small plateau, now—the angry and determined sounds of trained ski troops forming into a hunt and kill exercise. Another warmup, perhaps.

The "first snow" weekend lay but one night away.

And Mack Bolan was already having second thoughts concerning his ability to survive even these next few minutes.

14: FOR LIFE

Those guys obviously knew what they were doing, which was more than Bolan could say for himself. He was relying on instincts and quick reactions. They had the advantage of numbers, of familiarity with the terrain, and of trained military responses to the peculiarities of the situation.

The military use of skis was not exactly a new idea. The Lapps and the Finns had used them in the hunt as early as 3000 B.C., and there had been military applications throughout the recorded history of the frigid zones. The first ski manual of instructions was prepared by a Norwegian army captain in the early eighteenth century, and at about that same time and place, the first ski competitions were organized within the Norwegian military as a means of encouraging excellence among the troops.

No, it was not a new military idea. Only the sporting aspect of skiing was relatively new. These guys had a new twist, of course—the snowmobile—and they had obviously worked out some highly effective maneuvers and techniques to make the most of it. If they had seemed confused and vulnerable in that first contact, it was probably chiefly because they had not been entirely certain of the situation confronting them. They knew now, and not even the restricted visibility would stay them in their mission for long. All they had to do was to pick up Bolan's trail in the fresh snow, and the rest would be simple military precision. They had the advantage of numbers and terrain orientation. They would hem him in, run him down, and rub him out—one, two, three—as simple as that.

Unless . . .

The combat mind had instantly circumscribed the military situation existing on that stormswept plateau in the Rockies and seized a decisive plan of action. It was a long shot, but at least it was a shot.

"Change of plans," he told the lady, and ordered her off of the vehicle. "Which way to the lift house?"

She took her bearings from the slope and unhesitatingly pointed the way.

Bolan did not wish to leave a trail of footprints, from this point. "Get up on the vehicle and take a dive," he instructed her.

She understood instantly, complying without question.

It was a good one. He could barely perceive her landing point.

He carefully jockeyed the little buggy away

from the slope's edge and turned her about on a ninety-degree right angle to the previous course, then put her underway and jammed the throttle at half-open before leaping clear.

The snowmobile chugged on across the flatland and Bolan rejoined the lady. He sat in the snow beside her, Big Thunder up and ready in a two-hand grip—and again she understood, not moving, barely breathing.

Almost instantly another vehicle materialized along the backtrack and slid to a halt. Bolan could not see the men, but he could clearly hear their conversation.

"Damn! Did he go over?"

"Naw. Got out for a look-see then headed east. Fire three."

The girl beside him twitched as three quick shots were fired from that vehicle and the pursuit continued. The snowmobile chugged on out of sight, moving cautiously.

"What were they shooting at?" she whispered.

"Chase signal," he told her. "Probably geared to the compass points. Three shots means tracking east."

"What now?" she asked, moving that lovely face close to his.

"We hope," he replied, "it takes them a couple of minutes to learn they're tracking an empty vehicle. We find your brother and we find some skis—some nice light, cross-country skis. Then we head west, and hope to God you have a feel for the terrain around here."

"West is downslope," she reminded him. "Very hazardous in these conditions."

"Not as hazardous as east," he pointed out, and

helped her to her feet. "What sort of lift do you have?"

"It's a simple rope tow."

"Okay," he decided, "we'll take that route. You be thinking about where we go from there. I guess it's mostly in your hands now, Undy."

She did not reply, but moved off quickly toward the lift house.

And, yeah, Bolan felt that he'd known this lady for a long, long while.

The brother, Sondre, was something of a surprise to Bolan. Very young, perhaps eighteen or nineteen, a blond giant of a Norseman with very little command of the English language. He was understandably hostile and suspicious of Bolan, wretchedly cold, frightened, probably very hungry. He'd been bound hand and foot, covered with a light blanket, and left alone in the unheated building since early that morning.

The woman quickly explained the situation to him, using the native tongue, and the three moved hurriedly to the outfit shop for a selection of equipment and warmer togs for Sondre.

The procedure was consuming far too much time, and Bolan was trying to hurry them along when a mild argument erupted between brother and sister.

"What's the problem?" Bolan demanded.

"Sondre maintains we should not attempt downslope," she reported.

"Tell Sondre," Bolan replied heavily, "that the beast is east and west is best."

She smiled at that and relayed the advice to

her brother. He smiled, also, and gave a brief response in Norwegian.

"Sondre says—it is a paraphrase—go west, young man, and meet your maker."

If they could joke about it, okay, Bolan felt much better about the situation. They were a spunky pair, and they would need all of that they could muster. A sense of humor would not hurt a damn thing.

Another insurrection surfaced outside, however, as the three were linking themselves together on a life line. The wind was now beginning to howl and a premature nightfall was adding further complications to the environmental problem.

"What now?" Bolan growled.

"Mr. Bolan," Undy replied, picking her words tactfully, "Sondre is an Olympic skier. He insists that we will not survive the slopes in these weather conditions. The wind is rising. We could be in blizzard conditions at any moment. The others will be as hampered as we. They will be forced to call off the chase. Sondre knows of an overhanging rock ledge, nearby, where we may construct a snow cave and delay in safety."

There was wisdom in that argument, of course, but it was a limited wisdom, unmindful of some deeper truths. There was really no time for this discussion. Bolan knew his enemy, but he knew also that it would be impossible to thread the needle of survival unless all three were proceeding with a singleness of plan and purpose.

"Tell Sondre," he argued quietly, "—this, too, is a paraphrase—we have to run like hell where angels fear to tread. Our one advantage is the enemy's immobility. When it's safe for them to move, we cannot. Now it's got to be the devil or the deep blue sea. The mountain or their guns, which does he prefer?"

The kid did not smile at that translation. He threw down the life line and delivered an emphatic retort which his sister did not hasten to interpret.

"What'd he say?" Bolan growled.

"Sondre says—you are no different than the others. Guns and killing is your only life. He wishes no part."

Great. A beautiful speech, in almost any other situation. But not in this one.

"Do you share his feeling, Undy?"

She dug in her ski poles and stared straight ahead. "I do not wish their plan to succeed."

"Does Sondre understand the situation?"

"He understands."

"Tell him that I respect his decision to die a peaceful man. That does not mean, of course, that he will meet a peaceful death."

She told him, and the kid seemed to be wavering for a moment, but then he executed a beautiful kick turn, dug in his poles, and glided off across the flats, disappearing from view immediately.

The woman called after him in a faint voice, then turned pained eyes to the big grim man beside her. "He will die?"

Bolan nodded, and his voice was soft with regret as he replied, "It's not an Olympic game."

"You can save him?"

Probably not. He could, of course, die trying. It was not the fear of dying that gave Bolan pause but the relativities of responsibility. And what it boiled down to, finally, was the relativities of life itself. Was the life of the president more important than . . . ?

A guy could go on forever saving himself for some supreme moment, and commit an endless number of atrocities in the process. Or he could live his life as though each moment were a supreme one.

Bolan dropped the life line and told the goddess of the ski, "I can try, Undy. Go into the outfit shop and barricade the door. You'll probably hear a lot of commotion. If I'm not back shortly after that—go west, young lady."

Then *Skade* glided away to take on the beast of the east in open combat.

The great difference in men of similar talents lay not so much in what they did but why they did it.

Mack Bolan was a man who did what he *had* to do.

And, yes, there was a difference.

15: OPTIONS

The kid had been right about one thing, anyway. Gusting winds were howling across that plateau with force enough to give an almost horizontal movement to the falling snow, which itself was abating not a bit. Blizzard conditions were in the making and imminent. The wind chill factor was producing a dramatic effect upon the air temperature, a sub-zero effect. To all purposes, night had fallen. The trail left by Sondre's skis was barely visible, the impressions in the snow filling rapidly under the onslaught of wind and fresh snow.

Even the sounds of that frozen hellground were becoming muted, though no less intense. Bolan could still follow the play by ear, and it was quite obvious that the snortzenzoomer corps had already discovered the trail which Bolan was following.

And they were damned good, those guys. They

were literally running blind, yet obviously conducting methodical search patterns which had to depend entirely upon timing and perhaps a system of audible signals.

Bolan was reading the play as he tracked it, relying upon the story impressed upon the snowbed as well as the sounds in the air. He crossed the moment of initial contact—a double track of snowmobile disturbances crossing in a circle over the finer run of cross-country skis—a peel-out and reversal of direction by one buggy. And there was the pattern. They were ellipsing the track, running paired opposites to each other in an ever-widening pattern which would inexorably tighten an ever dwindling area of confinement for the quarry.

Another pair had jumped in, forty feet beyond the initial moment of contact. And now there were four running those shrinking elliptical patterns.

Bolan was beginning to understand their audibles, also. They were using engine sounds to signal turns and approaches, clutching in and revving the engine in number sequences—a precision drill team, running in the blind, and the drill was death.

Where the hell had they learned it? Not here, for sure—not this year—there had been no time since first snow to develop such skills. How long had these people been preparing for this mission?

Bolan's consciousness was evenly divided now—half of it reading the situation, the other half seeking a tactical solution. And, sure, there was a way to fight these guys. The largest problem was presented by Sondre, himself. Bolan could launch a grenade attack, targeting on their own audibles—but he would very likely end up killing the kid, as well, and where would be the profit in that?

No. He could not play it from the outside. He would have to pierce that elliptical shell of containment, enter the heart of it, get the kid beside him, and play the game from there.

And he had to do it in a matter of seconds.

He was running with the play, crouched almost double with his weight forward over the skis to read Sondre's tracks, isolated in the swirling atmosphere, the soft sounds of his own advance crushed by the moaning wind and zooming motors. The kid had slowed and perhaps halted completely, aware of his predicament and immobilized by indecision. Whatever the situation in there, Bolan had overtaken the center of activity and he was ready to make his move.

He timed the audibles for the crossing at the base of the new ellipse, then dug in his poles and leapt forward to thread the gap between the crossing vehicles. The machines were powering up his flanks to either side, at a distance of no more than ten to fifteen feet, closing up in the climb and sending position audibles to the other pair coming down from the top. Forty feet, then, from tip to tip, and closing constantly. They had their man in the pocket and they knew it. Any moment, now, the turkeyshoot would begin.

And then Bolan overran the crouching form of Sondre Wiegaard. The kid was waiting for him with the business end of a ski pole poised for the attack, and he came uncomfortably close to reaching his target. Bolan deflected the pointed steel with an arm block, following through with a no-mercy right to the chin, and the kid went limp.

So much for peaceful instincts. Any one who respected life would die fighting. Bolan hoped that the boy would remember that moment—or that he would live long enough to do so.

The time to begin the fight for life was before it was already lost. And perhaps the kid realized that grim truth now.

Bolan realized it—and knew the game well.

He removed the unconscious youth's skis and slid them toward the top of the pocket, then he primed a grenade for fast release, waited for the crossing audible, and heaved it toward the apex.

Not even that flash was visible except as a shimmery lightening closely contained within the gloom, but the blast eclipsed for a moment all other sounds of that noisy landscape—and one of them never returned. A single buggy was snorting around up there now, and it was no longer in the ellipse. A weak scream from the blast area announced, "I'm hit—I'm hit!"

The pocket fell apart completely at that moment. The two buggies at the lower edge exchanged a quick series of audibles and peeled away. Automatic weapons fire instantly laced into the zone from three sides, triangulating and sweeping in methodical patterns.

The turkeyshoot, yeah—but not exactly as it had been desired. The "pocket" no longer existed and there were options available to a knowledgeable warrior.

Bolan had the kid on his shoulder and he selected his option at the very moment that the firing began, gliding out between the two most promising firing angles into the null zone. He fired a single round from the AutoMag and kept moving, drawing the triangulated fire to that point just vacated. A few seconds of pinpointed fire was all he needed for success in the breakaway. He would have had that success but for a disturbing new element suddenly added to the game—a new sound, a new presence—the groaning and clanking of heavy armored units moving into position directly across his path of retreat.

He went immediately to ground, burying both himself and his burden in the snow as an instinctive reaction to that new threat.

When he looked up, a half-track armored scout car was standing beside him. A powerful carbon-arc searchlight blazed into brilliance and began sweeping the target zone, cutting through the pall effectively though not perfectly. An electronically amplified voice loudly commanded a cease-fire. Bolan stayed put, realizing that he was in the best of possible places, for the moment.

The snowmobiles shut down, presenting an eerie silence broken only by the howling and moaning of the wind sweeping that plateau.

The PA blared again, and this time Bolan recognized the Arkansas drawl of Captain Frank Harrelson. "What've you got here, Lieutenant?"

The snowmobile voice of command which Bolan had heard earlier responded promptly from nearby in the blind zone. "We think Bolan. The woman is missing and three of our men are dead, three wounded, maybe more by now. One of our light units is knocked out."

"So what're you doing about it, Tom? Throwing snowballs at 'im?"

"We had him in the zipper, sir. Just before you came up. I swear, this guy just doesn't make sense. It seems that he's broken out again."

"Correction, Lieutenant. He broke *in*. Bolan? Mack? You can hear me. I know you're here, Sergeant. Look, we tried. Okay? Now we're running out of time. Enough fun and games. I have a proposition for you. This is Frank Harrelson. Captain Harrelson. Hey, Grunt—we had our moments, didn't we? We can do it again. Let's white flag it. A ten-minute truce. We have a lot to talk over."

Sure. Bolan knew all about Frank Harrelson's white flags. They had a habit of turning red, very suddenly.

"No tricks, Sergeant. Look, I can let you lay out here and freeze to death, if that's what you want. You're not going to break clear, you know. I have a ring of steel around this plateau. But, hey, Sarge, you're pinning down my elite force. I need to move it on. The fun is over. Now it's time for work. I'd like to have you on my side. What do you say, hawg? You want to lay out here and turn to ice?"

There was a possibility, of course, that the guy was straighting it.

"I could put you to good use, boy. I've got myself a sharpshooter but he's not nearly as good as you. I can make you a rich man overnight."

Hell of hells, the kid was coming around. Bolan rolled atop him and placed a hand over his mouth, then guided an outflung hand to the cold steel tread of the scout car.

Harrelson was continuing with his pitch. "Filthy rich. And I can make you a general, if you'd like that. Sergeant to general in one easy step, one easy decision. What do you say, hawg?"

Bolan was not saying a damn thing. Nor was the kid. He was fully awake and aware now, quickly on top of the situation, squeezing Bolan's hand to let him know.

"I just can't understand this dumb shit you've been into, Sergeant," Harrelson went on, in that deceptively folksy tone. "I understand and respect your motives, but, dammit, boy, you're spinning your wheels against the tide of time. Who needs it? Who even wants it? They got your picture hanging in every post office in the country. They're going to shoot you down like a dawg, first chance they get. It's a waste, such a shameful waste. You need to come in with people who appreciate what you have to offer. We got a real interesting wingding going here. Hey, you know, I can't just sit here and talk at you forever, boy. I guess, uh, Mrs. Sanderson already filled you in, huh? Listen, she doesn't have it all. She even got the wrong slant. We're not assassins, Sergeant. You know what we are. We're a military force and we're on a military mission. I think you'd be interested in it. Course, if you'd rather be a frozen side of beef, well, I can respect that, too, I guess. To each his own, eh. I can only give you another minute. Hey—remember Sin duc Huong? We could do it again, you and me, together. I'll give you sixty seconds to think it over. White flag. Start your count."

Yes, Bolan remembered Sin duc Huong. And he was having no piece of Frank Harrelson—not until the moment of his own choosing.

A couple of eerily quiet minutes later, the searchlight was extinguished. The scout car's engine cranked up. Another voice on the PA sent the order to the ski troops: "Button up and put it away. Let the smartass have his frozen turf. Evacuate all wounded to the rear. Coffee and sandwiches in the snack wagon. Well done, boys, well done."

The vehicle lurched forward then spun in a sharp turn. Boland felt the kid stiffen and clutch at himself but he did not know why until the scout car clanked away and the snowmobiles withdrew. The caterpillar tread had passed over Sondre's right leg, burying it in harshly compacted snow—but only the snow had saved him from a mangling. There was simply no language communication possible, but Bolan knew that leg was hurt and hurting. He carefully dug it out and probed for obvious misalignments. Finding none, he cautioned the young Viking with a finger across the lips and hoisted him in a fireman's carry, then set off quietly in what he hoped to be the general direction of the outfit shop.

Only one thing appeared certain now. The kid would not be doing any skiing for awhile.

Nor, it appeared, would Bolan.

Whatever else Frank Harrelson may be, the guy was no idiot. He had not withdrawn from the field of combat as a special grace to an old war buddy.

The guy had meant what he said.

The head of Mack Bolan had lost primacy in the Colorado kill zone. Apparently it was enough, now, to merely contain him in a limited area. Which could only mean that the "other" hit was on, and moving into the countdown.

The Killer Force had proved itself, to someone's satisfaction.

And it was shaping into a bitter, bitter night in the kill zone.

16: COCK A WHITE HAT

"Sondre thanks you for risking your life to save him."

"Tell Sondre I like his guts. They were worth saving."

The lady gave Bolan a smile which could have meant many tender things. She lowered her eyes as she told him, "Undy thanks you, also, Mack Bolan. We both regret Sondre's unkind words to you, earlier. You are not like the others. You are quite different."

She hurried away before Bolan could respond to that, returning to the ministrations to the injured leg. They had built a bunk for the boy behind the counter of the outfit shop, the least drafty spot in the small building, and bundled him warmly against the deepening cold. The leg was not that badly damaged, as far as Bolan could determine, but it was painfully bruised and scraped from the knee down. The kid was about half sick, as well, a bit feverish—probably a result of the daylong imprisonment and exposure to the cold.

Things could be a lot worse, of course. And they could get a lot worse. Harrelson had withdrawn to a chosen perimeter simply because there was no military advantage in a blizzard. Almost any confrontation would be a one-on-one situation, and in any such situation, he must have figured that Bolan would have the better chance for survival. Harrelson was too good a soldier to spend men for nothing. He could afford to pull back and wait out the storm, inviting Bolan to then take the initiative, knowing full well that the advantage would then pass to the defense.

No, the guy was no idiot.

Bolan found some kindling in a bin and built a small fire in the potbellied stove.

"Is it safe?" the woman asked him.

"No," Bolan replied, smiling, "but it's a lot more comfortable. Isn't it?"

She replied with a smile and held her hands to the warmth.

"The wind is coming from the northwest," Bolan elaborated. "That means it's at their backs. They won't smell the fire, and I doubt they would see the smoke if they were standing right outside. I think it's safe enough, for now. Enjoy it while you can."

"I have tea, and a pan," she said, still giving him the warm smile. "And with a yard filled with—"

Bolan held up a hand and said, "Say no more. Best idea I've heard all day." He dumped the contents of a small metal trash can into the fire then stepped outside and filled the can with snow.

It was dry stuff with very little water content—excellent for skiing but not for much else. He had to make another trip outside before they had enough water for tea, and it was during that latter excursion that he thought he noted a lessening of weather activity. He did not mention it to the woman but made several trips to the window while the tea was brewing.

She told him, without looking.

"The storm is waning."

Bolan nodded agreement with that. "Wind shift, too. The front has passed."

"What will you do?"

He grinned. "I'll have some of that tea."

"What will you do?" she repeated, handing him a hot tin bowl.

He sipped it carefully, savoring the warmth and delicate flavor, then told her, "That's very good, Undy."

"What will you do, Skade?"

Bolan chuckled soberly. "I'll have to watch the conditions very closely and try to get the scouting jump on them."

"What does this mean?"

"Well, it's been a game of blindman's bluff. We both know the other is here—but not precisely where. War is a precision game. He who knows best usually does best. I need to find them before they find me."

"I see. You mean to attack."

"I must attack, Undy. It's the only hope."

"You could go west, Skade. You could do it now, as you could have done before."

Bolan shook his head to that. "That's no longer an option."

"Because of Sondre and me?" She delicately shook her head. "The option remains."

Their gazes locked above the tin bowls as he told the woman, "No way, m'lady."

"We will do quite well. You must escape and defeat the plot."

"You will be quite dead, both of you, and there's no certainty that I could make it on my own. I've done very little downhill skiing and I'm unfamiliar with the terrain. I could be still wandering around those wilds out there while they're burying the president. Or dead in a snowbank, myself."

She dropped her eyes and quietly told him, "I do not cherish life at the expense of such a man as you."

"And Sondre?"

"I speak for the two of us. Sondre could not dance upon your grave."

Bolan put the tea down and lit a cigarette. He offered it to her and she declined. He asked, "Ever have the feeling, Undy, that you're repeating some long forgotten experience?"

"*Dejà vu?*" she replied, wrinkling her nose at that. "Do you accept reincarnation, then?"

He grinned and told her, "I don't reject it. But I wasn't speaking of that. I just have the feeling that we've known each other before—you and me."

She said, "Yes, it is a comfortable feeling. I felt it immediately."

"How do you explain it?"

"I don't. I simply accept it. Gratefully. How do you explain it?"

"Time out of sync," he said, smiling soberly.

"I don't understand."

"I don't either." He laughed and reached out to squeeze her hand. The squeeze grew into something prolonged, and warm, and very special.

She whispered, "Please, I am very susceptible."

So was Bolan, but it was no time for that sort of thing. He let her go and returned to the tea, then went to the window for a weather check, then to Sondre for a patient check. The boy was asleep. The wind was dying. And Mack Bolan's time was running out. No, it was no time for . . .

He went over and pulled her to her feet, took her into his arms, held her tenderly. "Time out of sync," he explained huskily, "is life on the heartbeat. It's speed time, between the frames. You don't move along with it. You hover above it, and watch it pass—in any direction you choose. I can't explain it any better than that, Undy, but I loved you the moment I saw you. And it's enough, for me—understand? My whole life is out of sync. One heartbeat can expand to fill a lifetime. Does it make any sense?"

Her cheeks were awash with tears. "Yes. Yes, it makes much sense. I thought perhaps it was because I have been so alone but I—just hold me, please. Hold me."

He held her, and it was enough for two very lonely souls.

They moved together to the window. Bolan said, "Ten minutes, maybe."

She said, "It outweighs—I—I thought, for the past two years, that I had come to this country to realize a dream, only to find a nightmare . . . to—to see my husband killed. Such a waste, Mack Bolan. What do you call that kind of time—two years of nothingness?"

"How did he die?"

She sighed. "Realizing a dream. Lars was a champion skier. We came here to find the American dream. Opportunity, progress, dignity. But we were losing it all. So Lars began taking outside work. He was with the avalanche patrol one day and . . ."

"And what?"

"The mountain killed him."

Bolan told her, "Then he died doing what he loved best. Right?"

"I suppose that's right."

"How'd you get tangled up with Frank Harrelson?"

"Who is Frank Harrelson?"

"The beast of the east," Bolan said.

"Oh. The southerner. Sondre found them camped below our slope, one day. They took him into custody. Treated him badly. A few weeks ago, the southerner returned—supposedly to offer an official apology. But then, last week, they returned in force and stayed. Sondre and I became prisoners in our own home."

"What have they been doing here, Undy?"

She shrugged. "Plotting, scheming, practicing their games."

"In the snowmobiles?"

"Yes."

"Without snow?"

"They brought snow machines with them. You know? Artificially created snow? The temperatures have been suitable, especially at night. One reason they selected our site is that the sun's rays do not strike directly. They were able to maintain a frozen layer. Yes, they have practiced weeks with the snowmobiles. At first, surreptiously on our lower slope. Then, for the past week, brazenly—with Sondre and me confined. We thought at first they were genuine army soldiers. When they took us prisoners in our own home, we knew differently. This does not occur in America."

"Let's hope it won't be occurring again," Bolan growled. "What can you tell me about Harrelson?"

"Very little. He spends very little time at Snow Trails. The lieutenant, Thomas, has been in charge here. The southerner pops in and out, usually by helicopter. They plot and scheme briefly, and out again he departs. I can tell you that he is a wicked man—the beast, yes."

"And the others?"

"Not so bad as the southerner. Very firm and officious, yes, but also very proper. Very soldierly."

Bolan sighed and said, "Yeah. Very soldierly. That is precisely my problem. Those guys are good soldiers, well disciplined. How far away is Vail, Undy?"

"By highway, in good weather, perhaps ninety minutes."

"And by air?"

She nestled her head on Bolan's shoulder and replied, "By air, I do not know this. But the president does not visit Vail this year, if that is your thinking."

"Yes, that was my thinking. Where will he be, then?"

"This year he visits Berthoud Pass, as special guest of—"

Bolan stiffened to attention and interrupted with a growl. "That's just south of here!"

"Yes. We are adjacent."

A brilliant new light was illuminating the kill zone, it was a light within Bolan's own mind, and he was mentally chastising himself for leaping to military conclusions without properly circumscribing the facts. He had initially assumed that Snow Trails was part of the suck plan—then, with the input from Undy Sanderson, that it had figured chiefly as a training area and only secondarily as a suck station. But now, with ground zero revealed at a point a mere few minutes removed, the Sanderson resort was occupying a front line position—the jump point itself—and suddenly it had all come together, the time frames slipping into place, the picture resolving itself into a startling landscape of military determination.

"I have to get to my vehicle," he told the lady. He hurried over to rouse the sleeping youth, felt his head, and called back to the woman: "Tell him we're buying that snow cave. I'm tucking you both away for the night, then I'm jumping off."

Jumping off, yeah—maybe straight into the pits of hell. And time out of frame could, for damn sure, screw a guy up. It had all been there, from the beginning, looking at him from the disconnected pieces of the jigsaw puzzle scattered across the infinite floors of time.

A suck plan, sure, in which Bolan was both the sucker and the suckee. A regional strike force, yeah, with every law enforcement agency in the area tied up and roped in for the hunt on Bolan's head—a military diversion plan, dammit, pure and simple, nothing else. Even the treasury boys, according to Brognola, had been siphoned off to the preoccupations of the Bolan chase, while a formidable military machine geared itself for the primary strike.

So how many personal bodyguards customarily accompanied the president on his jaunts around the country? How many could trot along the ski slopes with him? What sort of actual protection could the presidential detail offer against combat troops and military armor?

Bolan had not been able to figure the mob's interest in all this. Why, for God's sake, hit the president? For what possible profit? But, then, the other question had kept edging in, also: why a military force? why all this commitment of arms, money, and men? why a military combat team if the only goal is to assassinate an individual? A sharpshooter could do the job, especially out here on these "big sky" slopes, with much more precision and certainty. Why make a military operation out of it?

What was it Harrelson had "offered" during that one-way conversation in the blind zone? A general's stars? In what army? Had the guy really been straighting it?

The answers banging around inside Bolan's skull were all too wild, too grotesque, entirely too far out to even merit consideration—but they were there, dammit, and they had arisen from the puzzle itself. He had to consider them, and he had to find a few more pieces to the puzzle.

The diversion had undoubtedly worked. Bolan had seen at first hand the total mobilization of police forces, down on the flats, and Brognola had confirmed that someone had engineered a minor bureaucratic miracle to get all those diverse offices marching together.

A diversion of another sort, also, had almost immobilized Bolan himself. And, no, Frank Harrelson was no idiot. He must have assumed that Bolan had taken the two civilians under wing. He'd obviously known Bolan better than Bolan knew himself. The sucker in the white hat would find himself torn between the dictates of conscience—and, yeah, the black hats always exploited that weakness of civilized men.

Except that it was not really a weakness.

Bolan might have gone floundering off into the blizzard, defying hostile and unfamiliar mountains, and thus taken himself completely out of play—except for that commitment to a couple of helpless civilians.

But, sure, Harrelson had read it as a weakness. So, give the smartass his conscience on isolated turf, let him play big brother and nursemaid to the weak and needy while the killer force moved into final position for the payoff strike.

But the "cornpone colonel" from Arkansas had been guilty of a basic miscalculation of human nature, especially of Mack Bolan's human nature.

There was more than one way to cock a white hat.

And Bolan knew all the positions.

17: FOR THE DEAD

The wind had calmed and the snowfall slackened to a moderate drop. The stuff was light and powdery and seemed to hang suspended in the calm air. The temperature had dropped dramatically, as well, and Bolan found the face mask entirely comfortable. He did not look too unlike the sentries who glided silently about the plateau in hooded parkas with snow clinging to them everywhere, but he did not wish to push too far in that direction. These troops were playing the game the way it was written; undoubtedly they had recognition signals and other means of ready identification.

Visibility was fair now. Objects could be seen from a distance of about a hundred feet, clearly defined at fifty feet. Lights were showing here and there, voices drifted across the flats, men were in motion in and around the house.

Bolan had not suspected that any of this would be quick or easy. His game was necessarily a soft one, depending entirely upon patience and perserverance. Each minute spent, though, was a minute for the other side. He could not afford to probe and reconnoiter the entire night away. Yet he had known also that the quiet game was the only one available to him—and the longer he played it, the more certain became that understanding.

Two full hours had elapsed since he'd tucked Undy and her brother into a safe womb and bade them farewell. During that time, he had scouted the forward perimeter and ascertained that it was, indeed, seemingly impenetrable. Ski patrols with walky-talkies were manning the slopes above the plateau. And there was very little slope up there, a football field's length, perhaps. Wheeled vehicles patroled the top. The narrow roadway, leading up to U.S. 40 a quarter-mile away, was blocked by a half-track. Elsewhere the plateau ended at vertical cliffs which would defy the most determined Alpine climber.

No quick and easy solutions, no, for sure.

He had considered and rejected several. One: to seize a scout car and blast his way out, crumpled under the argument that he could not both drive and blast at the same moment. The scouts carried 37 millimeter cannons, which was firepower enough, and they held their feet good in the snow—but they were not one-man vehicles. The other cars were fully crewed, and their feet would be just as good on the snow as Bolan's. He would not get far.

Another rejected plan was to rush the house, blast it with grenades, put a pistol to Harrelson's head and allow *him* to clear the way out. There was no assurance, though, that Harrelson himself would survive the grenade attack. And there was no assurance that the plot against the president would die with Harrelson.

For the moment, the quiet game was all Bolan had.

He could but wait and watch, bide his time, and seize whatever opportunity might arise.

At ten o'clock he watched the search parties begin their move against the lift house and outfit shop, and again he found reason to respect their military craft. No sloppiness there, no amateurish adventuring, but methodical execution of a soldier's job. Afterward, he listened to their reports regarding the warm stove in the outfit shop, the pan of tea, the evidences of habitation. They also found the false trail downslope which Bolan had carefully manufactured, and he took heart in their reaction to that.

"Looks like they went down the mountain, Lieutenant."

"How long ago?"

"Had to be after the front passed. From the degree of fill, I'd say maybe two hours ago."

"How long have you been skiing, Arnold?"

"Seven years, sir."

"Would you tackle that mountain tonight?"

"By choice? No, sir."

"Don't worry, I'm not sending you. I was just trying to measure the degree of desperation that sent them that way."

"I'd say pretty desperate, Lieutenant. I'd call it one chance in a hundred just for survival. And if they survived the slope, then there's still . . ."

A third man joined the conversation. "They're

nowhere, Lieutenant. One of them is hurt, too. We found blood on a makeshift bunk in the tack-room. I'd say a leg wound and I'd call it Bolan. Looks like the other two were doctoring him. They built a fire right under our noses and rode out the storm. Then they split as soon as the visibility improved. That kid is a whiz on skis, I hear. Picked up an Olympic medal when he was only fifteen. But I'm with Arnold. I wouldn't challenge that mountain tonight if I had a chest full of medals. And sure as hell I wouldn't try to crutch along a wounded man."

"Very well. Resume your patrol, Sergeant. Rotate your men at fifteen-minute intervals. We'll set up a two-section watch at midnight. I want all hands fresh for the push off."

"Aye, sir."

Bolan read a glimmer of opportunity unfolding, from that exchange. He continued the quiet watch, with "Sergeant Arnold" as the focus of that watch.

The moon broke through the deteriorating overcast an hour later. By that time, Bolan had a pretty good ear to the military posture of that base camp. The guys were beginning to relax, toning down, coming off the high moment, settling and looking ahead to the adventures of the morrow. He followed the "rotation" of the ski patrolmen with an ear to their recognition signals—and, at thirty minutes before midnight, he took a "warm break" with them, joining two other cold-numbed skiers for hot coffee and cigarettes at the snack wagon.

By midnight, the enemy had increased its numbers by one—and the new recruit was one of those volunteering for "first watch—Alpha Section."

The new sergeant of the guard was a guy called Scovic. He and the new recruit hit it off immediately when the latter quietly suggested a "layered command" for the onerous duty of checking the guard.

"We can alternate the rounds. I'll take the first one."

"Sounds okay, yeah. What'd you say your name is?"

"Pulaski. I'm on Arnold's team."

"Oh yeah. Okay, Pulaski, move 'em out and keep 'em on their toes. Mine are about froze off and I guess theirs are, too." The sergeant happily removed himself to the command van and "Pulaski" began the posting of the guard.

There really was a Pulaski, a very tired and cold young man with a constantly running nose who unwittingly had shared coffee and conversation with Mack Bolan before trudging off to a warm bunk and a couple hours of deserved rest.

And now the substitute Pulaski was posting the enemy's guard, setting their posture for the next two hours and—hopefully, the universe willing—for the rest of their lives on earth.

The Executioner had made his opportunity. The rest would be in the hands of whatever force shaped human destiny.

It was two o'clock on a blustery Washington morning when an official government limousine pulled beneath the canopy at National Airport. A heavily bundled figure with hat tugged low and coat collar turned up hurried from a darkened alcove and jumped into the rear seat. The limousine continued on around the exit ramp as Leo Turrin nervously lit a cigar and told his primary contact: "This one is a gut buster, Hal. I had to come."

"I know," Brognola replied.

"Who's your driver?"

"He's okay. What's too hot for the hot line, Leo?"

"They've got bugs on your telephones."

"Hell, I know that."

"*All* your telephones, Hal. I had the rare privilege a few hours ago of listening to a playback from your scrambler line."

"How are they getting it?"

"You tell me, buddy. All I know is, they're getting it. You've got a leak at NSC."

The electric tension in the atmosphere of that vehicle had stepped up considerably but Brognola was showing none of it in his voice as he replied, "Diminishing returns."

"What?"

"It's the point we've reached in government. You've heard of the rise and fall of civilizations? That's how it happens. It gets too big, too unmanageable, too ungovernable. And you reach the point of diminishing returns. That's where we're at, Leo. Systemized paranoia. Nobody trusts anybody. We all suspect everybody. When everybody's doing it, how the hell do you know which ones have the right and which don't? You don't know, that's the answer. The automatic checks and balances are gone, they don't exist. Big Brother is everybody."

"Okay. But the Big Brother I'm talking about is Augie Marinello. And he has access to the most sacred conversations in this town. You'd better find the hole."

"Maybe I already have," Brognola muttered. "What do you hear from Bolan?"

Turrin bit savagely into his cigar and muttered an unintelligible reply.

"What was that?"

The little guy removed the cigar, sighed, and said, "I'm afraid we've lost him, Hal."

Brognola put a hand to his forehead and leaned forward in the seat. "How do you make that?"

"He missed all the scheduled contacts over the past twelve hours."

"There's a blizzard in Colorado, Leo."

"Not for the past five or six hours. The pilot on that plane I just came in on says there are stars over Colorado at this moment. It's clear and calm. Most noticeable of all, Hal, there are no fireworks over Colorado—and there haven't been since mid-morning. It is now midnight in the mountains. Two hours ago, the old men in New York were dancing a jig on a proxy grave. They dumped ice cubes on the floor, Hal, and gave the traditional toast to a fallen enemy."

Brognola muttered, "Goddammit. That's what you really came to tell me, isn't it."

Turrin sighed. "I guess so. We knew it had to come. We knew the guy couldn't do it forever, Hal. But Goddammit—Goddammit—!"

The driver caught Brognola's misery in the rearview. He cleared his throat and started to say something, then changed his mind.

"Get it off your chest, Parker," Brognola growled.

"I'm not buying it, sir. They've danced over his

grave a couple of times before. I'm not forgetting Vegas, sir."

"It's different this time," Brognola muttered. He opened his briefcase and handed a file to Turrin. The *capo mafioso* switched on the reading beam and studied the report in silence.

His eyes were grim when he handed it back.

Brognola quietly said, "He was facing an entire army of Mack Bolans out there, Leo."

Turrin unashamedly dabbed at his eyes with the corner of a handkerchief. "Too bad that isn't true," he said. "The world could use a few hundred Mack Bolans. Now there are none. So what do we do about the imposters? How do you approach a force like that, Hal?"

"Very carefully," the fed replied through wooden lips. "There are, uh, delicate considerations of government. I believe it deserves cabinet-level response, if my suspicions are solid. The president is out of town."

Turrin made a disgusted sound deep in his throat and asked, "Where is he now?"

"Mixing business with pleasure in California. Goes on to Colorado tomorrow on a family holiday."

"Isn't that ironic."

"Yeah. The treasury boys have been eyeing that situation out there." Brognola cast an oblique glance of the eyes at his companion. "Maybe they have a hotline to the battle zone that I don't have. Early this afternoon they were considering a recommendation that the president bypass the Colorado date for the present. A few hours ago they scrapped that recommendation."

"Maybe it was just a weather watch," Turrin suggested.

"That, too, but you know how nervous they get over potential fireworks. No—I think somehow they got the word on our friend."

The little capo from Pittsfield sighed heavily. "Hal, I haven't tied one on in seven years. I think I'm due. Can I borrow a bedroom from you? And a couple of bottles?"

"First, let's talk about my bugged telephones."

"You're a cold-blooded shit, aren't you."

"I try to be. I'll cry tomorrow, Leo. For now, I need—"

Turrin again sighed and withdrew a folded paper from his inside coat pocket. "This will cover it. And if you insist on a working wake, I have another little item of possible interest. Gold."

"What?"

"I said, gold, the yellow stuff, the rare metal that turns the world on. Where do you suppose the old men are planning on finding a billion bucks worth of the stuff?"

Brognola fluttered his eyes and said, "Come again?"

"A billion—one thousand millions."

"What are you saying?"

Turrin slouched deeper in the seat and gnawed at the tip of his cigar. "I don't know what I'm saying. Except that the flap of the hour, at the New York headshed, is how best to handle, store, and convert one billion bucks worth of shiny yellow metal."

"Where the hell would they get that much gold?"

Turrin shrugged. "That's not the worry. I take it they already got it. The problem now is what to do with it."

"That's a lot of shit, Leo."

"It's a king's ransom, Hal. Now, if you want to work through the wake, I suggest you start looking for the king and wondering where the ransom is coming from."

"Are you talking about a snatch?"

"Naw, hell naw, I'm talking about one billion in gold. It was a figure of speech. Who could come up with a billion-dollar ransom? That's the whole point. This is for real, Hal. They've got a *gold* problem—a billion-dollar problem."

Brognola was giving him an odd stare. Turrin stared right back and asked him, "Do we keep gold reserves at the Denver mint?"

Brognola maintained the eye contact as he replied, "No. Is this billion bucks in gold tied somehow to the Colorado thing?"

"I believe somehow it's tied to Bolan's wake," Turrin said.

"How the hell could that be?"

Turrin's gaze wavered and fell. "I don't know. The bounty was up to a cool million bucks, but that was coming from all over and it's already in the hat. They don't need to bust gold to raise it, it's already raised. But the gold flap started, Hal, with the death dance."

"I wonder," Brognola said darkly, "if it's too late."

"Too late for what?"

"I once wanted to be a priest. Figured it was the only sure thing going. But I was very young, and I quickly got other ideas. Now, suddenly, I'm feeling very old. And I'm wondering if it is too late."

"It is," Turrin said, very soberly, "entirely too late. You wouldn't live long enough, cop, to hear out your own confession. Pick something surer. A locked room, say, and a good supply of booze."

Brognola looked at his watch as he sourly replied, "I'll drink to that, and to secret heroes, fallen comrades, and the fall of a civilization. Take it home, Parker."

And that, Turrin decided, was a fitting farewell toast to the damnedest guy either of them had ever known.

Let the world watch itself for a while.

The survivors were going to tie one on.

18: ENGAGEMENT

The "damnedest guy" was, at that very moment, tying on something of his own—but it was not a celebration of his own greatly exaggerated death.

One half of the Snow Trails force was maintaining the alert watch—split into two groups. The Alpha section patroled the inner compound area—the plateau itself. These were all ground grunts and ski-troops. Bravo section represented the motorized troops. They patrolled the approaches and overlooks—perhaps all the way to U.S. 40.

The other half of the force was crowded into the guest cabins, under orders to sleep and rest. And from the looks of those guys, the orders were totally unnecessary. They'd spent a tough day in harsh weather.

Bolan estimated the total force at about three hundred men, not counting the officers. And he readily acknowledged the fact that they would have to be regarded as elite troops—*real* soldiers with toughness of spirit, above-average intelligence, and a willingness to absorb personal hardships without complaint.

The discipline was amazing, considering the fact that it was a cosmetic force with no organizational authority other than that imparted by the men comprising it.

The organizational line, itself, was conventional enough, modeled along the team concepts of the modern army. Each team was small and self-contained, though strongly interlocked, in the operational sense. It was an army of line combatants which transported itself, supplied itself, supported itself; there were no logistics elements, *per se*, which Bolan could discern.

It was certainly no ragtag collection of street punks but a thoroughly capable and efficient combat force. They were taking nothing for granted and therefore offering no angle of exploitation which Bolan could see.

In a sense, though, this worked out as a plus for Bolan. He could place himself inside the skins of these men—think like them, feel like them, become indistinguishable in their midst.

And that was the only game he had.

Scovic was in the command van, taking his second tour of "warm relief" and going over the guard rosters. Bolan, *a la* Pulaski, was out cruising the compound on skis and looking for an angle. This was his second "inspection" of the guard posts and at least he was becoming a familiar figure—and an authoritarian figure—if nothing else. This alone would buy him nothing, of course. He could not stray far from the normal routine of the watch and he dared not risk too much in casual contacts with this highly professional enemy. He did still have a relative freedom, of course, and a mobility which could develop into some sort of effective game plan. Under the circumstances, things were going great. They just were not going there fast enough.

Prior to joining the enemy's ranks, Bolan had again rotated his personal armaments to concealment beneath the parka. He had six grenades, a few incendiaries, the AutoMag and six spare clips, the Beretta and four clips, the razor-edged stiletto, a couple of garrotes. All in all, against a force of some three hundred elite troops, not a hell of a lot.

But he was beginning, now, to reevaluate his position in the Colorado game. His entire thrust of the past several hours had been toward disengagement, withdrawal—a tactical retreat and a hotline to Washington. He'd been thinking like a scout who'd stumbled onto a secret enemy offensive—a forward scout, deep in enemy territory, struggling desperately only to extricate himself from enemy encirclement so that he could get the word back to command, to the main force.

Maybe the "angle" he'd been looking for had been in his own mind all the while. Maybe it was a matter of viewpoint, of personal vision, of role identification.

Why disengage?

Hell, he was here in the enemy camp, *part* of the enemy camp. He was not a scout, dammit. He was a guerilla force, in successful penetration of the enemy. *That* was the game, the only sensible one. Engagement, dammit, not disengagement. He could not get out to neutralize the plot. So okay. The only game left was to neutralize it from within.

With that decision, his thoughts returned immediately to the question of the armored vehicles. One was on patrol station at the exit road. The other two were parked beside the house, under guard by a sentry from the Bravo section. This guy was not in Scovic's detail and therefore not subject to the "warm rotation" enjoyed by the Alpha people. He was a sort of forgotten man, alienated by distance as well as territory from his own command. The guy had been given no relief since the setting of the midnight guard.

It was a likely place to start.

Bolan cruised past there and gave the guy a quick lookover. He was standing between the vehicles, arms crossed at the chest and huddling over them to conserve body warmth. Bolan returned immediately and skidded to a halt from a snowplow turn at the rear of the vehicles. The Bravo man was not wearing skis. He had tramped the snowbed between the vehicles into hard, icy compaction. The boots were caked with ice all the way up and the face mask was brittle with frozen moisture from his breath.

"You okay?" Bolan asked him.

The guys lips were so stiff that his reply was almost unintelligible. "I'll make it."

"I don't think so," Bolan told him. "Bravo forget you're down here?"

"I go off at two hundred hours. I'll make it."

"We have our people on fifteen-minute rotation. Look, man, this just isn't the way it's done. You go down to our snack wagon and put some hot coffee inside. I'll cover for you here. There's a foot warmer down there, too."

"Thanks, but I'd better stick."

"I'm ordering you, man. It may be your equipment, but it's my turf."

"You the sergeant of the guard?"

"One of them, yeah."

"Yeah, I've been watching you zooming around here. I thought you ski troopers had the hard duty. Now I'm wondering."

"I'm relieving you, Bravo. Take fifteen."

The guy came unstuck and shuffled forward. "Okay. It's your turf. If they fine me, though, you pay it. What's your name?"

"Scovic."

"Thanks, Scovic."

The Bravo man struggled off across the flats and Bolan immediately went to work. He raised the engine hoods and taped a grenade to each vehicle, then primed them and wired the release pins to the accelerator rods. It was a simple but effective booby trap. One pump of the gas pedal would detonate it. The resulting blast would easily disable the armored vehicles, but Bolan was going for a bit more than that. He also loosened each fuel line to a drip-leak then carefully concealed all traces of the tampering.

The guy was back in ten minutes, which was twice the time Bolan had required, and he was looking a lot better. Bolan told him so, adding: "Didn't hurt a bit, did it."

"Keep it between us, just the same," the guy said. "The man over there tells me you're not Scovic, though."

Bolan chuckled softly at that. "Scovic wouldn't mind paying your fine. Don't worry. It's between us."

"A sergeant can afford it. I can't. I have mine planned to the last dollar."

"Yeah? What are you going to do with yours, Bravo?"

"I'm going to lay in the sun for a whole year. I just figured it out. The Caribbean sun, rum and coke from a spigot, lots of crazy women."

"Have to watch those crazy women, Bravo. They'll suck up everything you have and leave you wondering where it went."

"No, I have that figured, too," the guy replied, very sober about it all. "I have a system. A budget. One thousand a week. That's all I break at a time."

"I guess that would run you a year," Bolan said lightly.

"Figure it again, Alpha. That will run me *twice* around the track."

Bolan did figure it, and he went away from there with a new sense of the magnitude of this operation. Twice around the track at a thousand a week was roughly *one hundred thousand dollars!* Was that the take, per man? For the common grunt, a payoff like that? He ran a fast mental calculation, figuring only three hundred men in the force and at the minimum pay, and his mind reeled under the result of that calculation.

Thirty million dollars? For nothing but personnel? And was it, then, a one shot deal?—hit and run?—collect and play for the rest of a lifetime with no further commitment to the force?

If that were true, then the stakes of this game had to be incredibly high. But who could—or even *would*—supply such a fat purse for a one-shot operation?

His mind returned again to a consideration of

the fantastic overkill in this mind-boggling game. And, again also, to Frank Harrelson's solo pitch via the PA system. How much was fact and how much oversell? General's stars and filthy riches, military forces and the politics of assassination versus *thirty million dollars* in one-strike hit money.

What the *hell* could it all mean?

He went straight to the command van, removed his mask, opened the parka, and sat down across the desk from Sergeant Scovic.

He was a man of about Bolan's age, hard around the eyes, a no-nonsense set to the mouth. Those eyes flattened as he glanced up from the paperwork and then came back to hold the fix. "Who are you?" he asked his assistant.

"I'm Pulaski," Bolan replied flatly.

"No you're not." That cold gaze was raking Bolan up and down. He started to push himself away from the desk.

"Don't do that," Bolan quietly commanded. The Beretta was there, watching the guy through the ominously bulbed silencer.

Scovic's hands stiffened flatly against the top of the desk. "Well, would you believe this," he said coldly.

Bolan said, "You'd better, Scovic."

"What do you want?"

"You."

Those hands twitched but remained where they were. "Okay. You've got me. Do it."

"I'm going to. Don't get any false hopes. I'm going to burn you, Scovic. End of game, for you. It will be quick and easy, you have my word on that. Anything you want to say?"

"Yeah. Die screaming, Sergeant."

"Is that all? With all the profit gone, you still want to burn your country?"

"My *country!*" Scovic jeered. "You're a nut, you know that? Cappie sure has you pegged. He'll nail you, too, dude."

"Let's stick with you. You don't owe anything to anybody, eh? You want to see it all burn."

"You have it turned around, Bolan. I don't owe. *They* owe. They owe all of us. Even you, sucker. You could have cut yourself in. Know that?"

"I never heard the size of the pie, Scovic."

Those lips twisted, sneering silently.

"Big deal," Bolan said coldly. "A few thousand in the hat—and for what? I run through that much in ammo every day."

The guy just sat there, staring glassily, the sneer hovering at those distorted lips—and that was the way it was when the Beretta chirped and opened a third eye between the glassy ones. This one bubbled red froth, and Scovic went over backwards, chair and all, dead before the fall.

Bolan sighed, wagged his head, and reached for the paperwork which marked Sergeant Scovic's final organized activity among the living.

It was a series of rough mathematical calculations, all based on a central figure of two hundred and fifty thousand. Bolan folded the paper and added it to his pouch.

"They owed you, eh?" he muttered.

So the going price for a sergeant's soul was a quarter million bucks.

It was some hell of a game, that much was sure. And these people were playing it with a vengeance. According to Scovic's calculations, he had drawn three "disciplinarian fines" of five thousand dollars each. No wonder the Bravo trooper was skittish about leaving his post. And it explained much about the tight discipline within the outfit. Their reward was apparently tied directly to their competence and dedication. Not a bad idea, at that.

Bolan dragged the body into a corner of the van and covered it with a blanket.

He really did not need to know the name of the game. He knew the rules, and that was enough.

And the game was definitely on, once more.

19: THE DANCE

Most of the lights had been extinguished in the house. Undy's home had obviously been transformed into a forward command post. The officers were billeted there, and it had been the center of operations throughout the long evening.

Bolan relieved the sentry at the front, sending the guy off on warm rotation. "Who's inside?" he asked, before the sentry left.

"Alpha leader, Bravo leader. Another troop I don't know."

"Looks like they're buttoned up for the night."

"Privileges of rank," the sentry replied philosophically.

Bolan removed his skis the moment the guy pushed away, then he went up the steps, opened the door, and went inside.

Only the living room area was lighted. Maps and combat charts lined the sloping walls. A folding blackboard on a tripod was set up beside the fireplace, bearing cryptic diagrams in several colors of chalk. The couch had been pushed aside and a powerful field radio console installed in its place.

And, yeah, this explained the limited access question. The house had been totally off limits to enlisted personnel since Bolan joined their ranks. He was standing in their war room.

He removed his parka and left it on a hook near the door—and he was standing at the blackboard, interestedly studying the colored diagrams, when a guy stepped in from the kitchen. A .45 was strapped to his hip on military web, his shoes were off, and he carried a glass of milk and a sandwich.

Lieutenant Thomas, Bolan presumed, of the snortzenzoomer corps—Alpha leader—a quick identification, via that gratingly unpleasant voice.

"What the hell are you doing in here, soldier?"

"Nice and warm in here," Bolan said, sizing the guy. Young, tough looking, all hardness and all business. These people, officers and men alike, seemed to be from a common mold.

"A thousand dollars worth of warm?" Thomas responded harshly.

Bolan got the meaning of that. Discipline by the dollar's worth, yeah.

"Heard you lost some men today," Bolan explained. He turned to face the guy, full on. "If you're looking for replacements, I'm volunteering."

Thomas was a bit uneasy with what he was seeing. He placed his food on a small table near the fireplace and came on with a scowl. Bolan noticed that the flaptop on the holster was open, the hand hovering there. Thomas's voice was a bit unsteady as he demanded, "What's your name, trooper?"

"Bolan, Mack Samuel. Master Sergeant."

Cool, yeah. The expression on that face changed not a quiver but the guy was coming on him like Genghis Kahn, and Bolan responded in kind.

He met him with a kick to the belly that *whoofed* the guy over and sat the guy down. He was upon him with a nylon garrote before that stunned diaphragm could begin a recovery.

Thomas died there, with one hand at his belly and the other clutching the throat—and he died quietly if not so quickly.

Bolan placed the body behind the couch and went immediately up the stairs to the sleeping level. He found a guy sleeping in the first bedroom and left him there with a slashed jugular. The one in the next room raised himself on his elbow in his bed as Bolan strode through the door. That one got to see what had come for him, but very briefly.

The Executioner wiped his blade clean on the bedsheet and went on without pause, but there were no others present on that upper level.

He left a marksman's medal on the landing and returned below for a thorough search of the ground floor but found none there, either.

The mysterious Captain Harrelson apparently did not sleep with his troops. Which was dammed good luck for the captain, but a disappointment to the wearied warrior from Pittsfield.

He took a pad and pencil from the field radio desk and made a sketch of the blackboard diagram then jotted several notes concerning the stuff on the walls.

He went back to the radio, sat at the desk, and undertook an examination of the communications rig. It had HF, VHF, and UHF capability—as well as what appeared to be a couple of landline terminals. He pursued that latter finding, discovering to his elation a junction with the house telephone line.

Which explained why they had smashed Undy's instruments instead of merely ripping out the line.

Bolan went to the front door and noted that the sentry had returned from his warmup. The guy was looking around in some confusion, obviously very much agitated. Bolan opened the door and called down, "Trooper!"

"Yessir?"

"It's okay. I'm briefing the duty officer on the patrols. You take over my rotation for the balance of the watch."

"I'm sorry, I—"

"It's okay, I'm relieving you. Give each man five minutes. Start where you are and work it clockwise around the perimeter. Got that?"

"Got it. Do I have . . . ?"

"You have the duty officer's direct orders. Carry them out."

The guy took off, a bit uncertainly. Bolan stood at the door until he saw the next sentry in line moving across the flats toward the snack wagon, then he went back inside and directly to the mobile radio station.

He found the secrets of the telephone system and patched in a line. Now, if only the storm had not taken the whole Rocky Mountain Bell system with it . . .

Parker returned from the all-night liquor store and put the bag of booze in the front seat, then walked around to climb in behind the wheel of the official limousine. He cranked the engine and swiveled his head to regard the two somber men occupying the rear seat.

He inquired, "You want to open it here or . . . ?"

"Or," Brognola growled.

Parker put the car in gear and eased away from the curb.

"It's wrong," the top cop muttered, a moment later. "We need to be doing something more constructive than toasting the dead."

"You tell me what," Turrin replied, "and I'll do it."

"We have a pentagon problem. We could start there."

"How high is the problem?"

"Two stars high," Brognola grumped. "That much for sure. It could go higher, though, and that's why I want to talk to the president before I flex a muscle."

Turrin was saying, "So why don't you fly?" when the mobile telephone beeped an incoming call.

Turrin conceded the floor with a gnash at his cigar and settled into the corner of the seat as Brognola sighed and took the call. "Juno Two," he announced.

An instant later, he stiffened and grabbed Turrin's leg in a hard squeeze. "Yeah, it's a safe phone. More so, probably, than any I've got." He flipped the call onto a speaker in the roof as he continued, "Where've you been, Striker? We've had you on the death rolls for hours."

Leo Turrin's heart was pounding as the tired, familiar voice clipped down from the ceiling. "I've been pinned down since just past noon. I may be on short time, so let's cover the business first. I'm at Snow Trails. It's the forward base for this paramilitary operation. But it's not the only base. I just learned that it's only one of three frontline commands taking part in the move. I'm inside Snow Trails and I think maybe I can neutralize this one. But you'll have to get some military up here—and I mean damn quick—to begin a sweep of these hills. Meanwhile, keep the president in Washington and put him in a bunker if he still has one. I have to—"

"What's that mean?" Brognola interrupted. "The president isn't even in Washington. He should be landing at Lowry Field most any minute, now."

"That's the air force base near Denver?"

"That's the one."

"What's the itinerary from there?"

"What's this all about, Striker?"

"The hit is on the president, Hal."

"Oh my God! Are you certain of that?"

"As certain as death itself. I'm sitting in the enemy's war room at this very moment. They're going to hit the president, unless you can find a way to stop it."

Turrin fidgeted, sighed, and made a hand signal to his companion.

"Sticker is here with me," Brognola told the incredible guy at the far end of that conversation. "He's glad you're alive."

"Me, too. Tell Sticker his guts were running true. This is the damnedest operation I ever fell into. Do you believe you can get a reaction going quick enough from that end?"

"I don't know. I've been thinking about it. I'm smelling a conspiracy to end them all, Striker, and I don't really know who to trust with this information. I have to—"

"Hell, just push all the buttons and let nature take its course. And I'll cover all I can from this end. What about that itinerary?"

"He'll be taking a chopper into the mountains from Lowry. Maybe I can catch him there."

"You should be able to catch him anywhere, Hal. He's never out of communications, is he?"

"Supposedly, no. In this case, I really couldn't say for sure. What's the plot? How are they turning it?"

"With three full scale combat units, including armor, ski troops, helicopters. Something is, uh, off key though, Hal. It's all too much for much too little. I don't believe they're going for a simple assassination."

"What are they going for, then?"

"It reads more like a snatch."

Brognola turned stunned eyes to his companion.

Turrin hissed, "The king's ransom!"

"Not just the president," Bolan was continuing, "but I think maybe the entire first family. Are they with him, Hal?"

"They sure are," the top cop growled.

"I don't read politics in anything I've seen," Bolan went on. "It's purely a money matter. How much do you suppose the traffic would yield? How much would the U.S. government be willing to pay for the safe return of the president and his family?"

"Try a billion bucks in gold," Turrin said quietly.

"We, uh, may have some input on that," Brognola told the soldier. "Sticker says the old men are already counting a billion in gold. Read that with a B—one *billion* in gold, Striker."

"Okay, that reads. It's the only thing that does. There's your conspiracy, Hal. How much is in a billion? My mind doesn't travel that far."

"A thousand millions," Brognola grunted. "And my mind doesn't either. But the boys over on Capitol Hill toss around multibillion figures as casually as ordering lunch."

"Turn the man around," Bolan said quietly. "If you can, send someone in his place. Let's smoke these people and end it, here and now. My time is up. Ringing off."

The overhead speaker clicked then buzzed with a dial tone.

Brognola pulled a card from the base of the telephone and immediately placed another call.

Parker's eyes were connecting with Leo Turrin's, in the rearview. Something flashed there, and the marshal said, "I told you about dancing on unmarked graves."

Turrin smiled wanly and replied, "Yeah. Well, this one has got to be the top of the order. Better save those bottles, guy. We may need them yet."

Leo Turrin's guts simply would not be still. The whole crazy caper was just too stunning to the senses. Imagine . . . a kidnap plot against the

President of the United States. Nothing was sacred, anymore.

Brognola was tensely drumming his fingers on the console, awaiting a priority connection.

"Civilizations have crumbled over less," he muttered with a sidewise glance at the little capo mafioso. "We can't let this happen, Leo. For God's sake, we just can't—" He broke off suddenly and cupped his mouth at the transmitter, speaking urgently in a hushed whisper.

Sure, it had gone to Brognola's guts, too.

And how, Leo Turrin wondered, about the iron man, himself? Would Mack Bolan run out of guts at the top of the order?

Guts, no. Heart, though—maybe so. And life. Yeah. The guy could very easily run out of life.

And if he did on this one, then an entire nation, and maybe the whole civilized world, would bitterly taste the severity of that loss.

Brognola was fuming with frustration, having a hard go at the telephone.

Turrin turned away from that agony—and turned within, to his own. The little underboss from Pittsfield who enjoyed ear at the councils of kings would be not a whit surprised if all communications to the president should turn up missing. Somehow Leo Turrin already knew that the die was cast and the wheel of fate was turning under its own power. The dons did not dance without good cause.

Brognola was not going to get through to the president.

A billion-dollar gold dance so proclaimed.

The only thing standing between the life and possible death of a nation was one lone soldier, an incredible guy whom the entire nation was trying to eat.

And what if that lone soldier should fail in his self-appointed task? The presidential family would be subjected to the uncertain mercies of a pirate band as well as the well-established viciousness of the Council of Kings.

And what if the government should refuse to meet the ransom demands. For God's sake, who would make that decision? And what if it came down on a hard line, no pay, no deal, no concession to terrorist blackmail? What would become of a nation which refused to bail out its own first family?

Looking at Hal Brognola's worried face, Leo Turrin had the answer to that. Yeah. Civilizations had crumbled over much less.

20: KILL ZONE: EVERYWHERE

The grimness of the situation was simply appalling.

It was almost time to change the guard. Seventy-five cold and edgy men were patroling that plateau on skis—fierce, professional soldiers with much at stake and apparently very little to lose. These men had tasted the hell that was Vietnam; if all were like the samples he had directly encountered, then they were a bitterly cynical bunch, who felt cheated at the game of life and shortchanged in the final accounting ... and they were going to collect in a hell game of their own making, this time, with a reward more befitting the sacrifices of the ordinary soldier at war. Yeah, a tough bag of cookies, and they would not crumble when the going became tough. And there were seventy-five more, just like them, who would be arising within the next few minutes and preparing to take their places in the night's grim watch.

Patroling above the plateau were the other half of the "Blue Force." Bravo Blue was the wheeled counterpart of Alpha Blue. One hundred and fifty strong, they were foot soldiers, mostly, heavy weapons men and civil containment teams in jeeps and personnel carriers. They also manned the three half-tracks, with the firepower of a light tank on each.

Bravo Blue's mission was to capture a town, a whole damned town. They would disrupt communications, neutralize the local police establishment, seal off all transportation routes, and hold the town securely until the completion of the overall mission.

Alpha Blue consisted of ten attack teams on skis and in snow buggies. They were the crunch force, the men up front. All carried light automatic weapons and side arms. Their mission was to neutralize the presidential security forces and to take physical custody of the president and his family.

Red Force and White Force were smaller peripheral units, already deployed, each a scaled down version of the larger Blue Force. If necessary, in a pinch, either of these could relieve or augment the primary units.

Each outfit in the operation carried both primary and secondary mission assignments—and there was even a fall-back "scramble" contingency plan in case everything fell to hell.

They'd thought of everything—and, yeah, these people knew the games of war.

Blue Force would be jumping off at four hundred hours. Which left Bolan two hours at best to try his own grim game of counterwar. And even if he could stop or disorganize this primary group, there were all those secondaries and contingencies to think about.

Appalling, yeah.

Even more appalling, though, was the thought of the President of the United States, his wife and children, prisoners or perhaps even casualties of such contemptible greed.

And casualties there might well be.

Bolan could not read it all in the sketches and diagrams of their war room, but what he could not read could be easily surmised. The overall plan, apparently, was to seize the small mountain town which had risen around the Berthoud Pass Winter Sports Area. It was there the presidential family were weekending. They would be taken into custody and held under house arrest, pending ransom negotiations. If all went well, the entire strike force would withdraw by air and with full assurances of safe conduct out of the country. One of the president's children would be taken along as a hostage to guarantee the withdrawal. There were contingencies, however, in the event that negotiations failed—in the event that there were "no surviving hostages," or in the event that the entire thing fizzled from the beginning.

There were, however, no contingencies for Mack Bolan. They had not reckoned with a one-man guerrilla army on the counteroffensive, and he was going to make them pay for that.

He had made a thorough study of their communications plan. It was displayed on typewritten cards taped to the field radio, even to authentication tables and coded emergency commands.

Now, with but two hours to blast-off, Bolan

donned the headset and punched in the armor channel.

"Bravo Blue, this is Blue Command. Situation One."

The powerful carrier from the scout car which had been deployed in the slot all night bounced an immediate reply in clipped tones: "Bravo Blue, aye. Go."

"Blue Command, Situation One." Bolan's finger traveled along the hours/minutes authentication chart. "Authentication, Zebra Alpha. Request immediate Apple Mary support."

"Roger, Blue Command. Bravo Blue is rolling with Apple Mary."

So okay, that would bring the scout car down out of the slot.

With a silent apology to Undy Sanderson's dreams, he threw a fire stick to the rear of the house, then quickly slipped into his parka, grabbed a chattergun from a rack at the door, and went out front to meet them.

Flames were licking along the sloped roof to the rear when the armored vehicle arrived. The gunner's hatch popped open and a bare head popped out. The scout commander called up to Bolan, "What have you got here?"

"We're under attack. I think that guy Bolan has come back. Take me aboard."

"Where is your Bravo duty officer?"

"He's a casualty. Take me aboard, dammit!"

The fire was drawing excited attention from around the compound. The dedicated Bravo sentry at the side of the house slid around the corner and yelled, "Sirs! I got two tracks parked back here!"

"Well move 'em out of there!" the scout commander bawled.

The cab door opened and another man jumped out to assist the sentry. Both men disappeared around the corner as Bolan ran down the stairs and stepped into the scout car.

He popped the two remaining men in there with a pair of quiet chugs from the Beretta and dumped the bodies into the snow at the front of the house, then took the conn and moved that prize quickly away from there.

The first booby trap detonated when he was about twenty feet out, a double explosion accompanied by immediate daylight and roaring flames. The other came a heartbeat later, with identical results, and both the vehicles were enveloped in flames.

Bolan saw one guy jump clear with his clothing aflame. A skier appeared from somewhere to grab the guy and throw him into the snow. Bolan thought of the sentry who dreamed of warmth and two lazy years under the sun, and fleetingly wondered if that was the one—but there were more pressing things to occupy his mind, and already he was putting that scene behind him.

He punched in the public address system and bawled the command: "All skiers to the slope! We are under attack! Skiers to the slope!"

He was aware of flitting figures gliding from all directions across that plateau, grim in their determination to repulse any invaders. He found himself admiring that reaction, respecting those men for what they'd once been regardless of what they had become, and an almost overpowering revulsion for the job ahead rose up in him.

He was in the position required now, though,

and it was no time for a softening of the combat spirit. He knew what he had to do—and by God he was going to do it.

He arced the steel-clad monster into pointblank range at the center of the cabin area and quickly went back to man the 37 millimeter cannon.

Those cabin doors were banging open and half-clad troopers were crowding onto the small porches for a gawking appraisal of the situation out there. One guy without shoes was floundering through the snow along that line, shouting something to the troopers on the porches.

The ammunition in the burning vehicles was starting to go and the fireworks were becoming really spectacular when Bolan rose up in the gun pit, struck the magazine, and commenced firing into that line of cabins.

Death walked the night watch on that frozen plateau, bringing unseasonal heat, searing flesh, flowing blood, the mad scramble for survival amidst flying bodies, screams and yells and choked-off commands, flames from a dozen burning buildings—and utter, unimaginable madness.

And then he shoved in another magazine, rotated the firing line to the western slope, and started all over again.

A guy came gliding in with an anti-tank rocket tube across the shoulder. Bolan took him with the .44 and went on with the kill.

And, no, there was no contingency plan to cover this.

The chattering of automatic weapons in return fire from the darkness grew less frequent and more isolated—and soon there was none. Some, probably, had decided to write contingencies on the spur of the moment and had taken the only sane course: down the slope. Those, Bolan would not worry about. The entire plateau was now a flame-leapt disaster area.

He secured the gun and returned to the conn, wheeled around, and headed out.

The radio was going crazy.

He picked up the mike and reported in.

"Bravo Blue, this is Apple Mary One. Recommend contingency situation three, repeat, contingency three. Alpha Blue is in full retreat. Blue Base has fallen. All Apple Marys are disabled or destroyed. Suggest total radio silence, contingency three. Apple Mary One is signing off."

There was no response whatever to the report.

Contingency Three was the total scratch plan.

Bolan sent the scout on up the drive and into the slot.

Bravo Blue, also, was in full retreat. He remained clear and watched them go, then followed the line of vehicles to the highway. The line turned north at that point. They were running for Mt. Audubon, and that was good. Bolan turned south, running for Berthoud Pass.

And that was good, too.

The snow plows had been busy. The highway was clear and fully navigable—although, at this hour, there was no traffic whatever but for that "military" convoy running smoothly north.

Bolan found the VHF command net on the scout's radio, and punched in. A carrier with helicopter background noises was just completing a cryptic instruction on that channel. Bolan barged into there with a contingency of his own.

"Force Command from Apple Mary One. Do you read? Over."

And, yeah, the cornpone colonel was there. In the chopper.

"Forget it, Sergeant. I'm reading you loud and clear."

"It's a busted play, Captain. Tuck it in and take it home."

"Way ahead of you, Superhawg. You better grow eyes in the back of your head, dude. That's where you're going to need them for the rest of your life."

Bolan chuckled tiredly into the microphone. "We can do it right now, Captain. I'm on U.S. 40 just south of Blue Base. Feel like trying for all or nothing?"

The guy laughed back at him. "Thanks, I'll pick my own battlefields. It's a shame, hawg. A real cottonpicking shame. Know what our share was? You can't count that high. Five hundred million. Believe it? We had it proofed and damn near spent. See what you missed? Well, it was my error. Didn't know you'd grown into such a damned jar head. A few hours ago, hawg, I gave you the opportunity of a lifetime. You could have come in for fifty mil."

"I can't count that high, either, Trooper," Bolan replied.

The guy sneered at that. "There's no idiot like a superhawg. Your friends in New York told me I'd have to take you first. I guess that was my first error. I really didn't buy that."

"You tried it, though."

"Sure. To keep peace in the family. It was part of the deal. And I damn near got you, soldier."

"Damned near isn't good enough in this game, Captain. You know that. What was the rest of the deal? You really expected those old men to play with you once they had their hands on all that gold?"

It was a simple probe into the mechanics of the plot, but it paid.

The guy laughed it off but told Bolan what he'd wanted to know. "There are checks and balances, even in the super world." Which simply confirmed, to Bolan's mind, that the mob had engineered the conspiracy and had planned to sluice the ransom into usable channels—a *commissione* specialty.

The radio signal from the chopper was fading rapidly, the distance between the two men ever widening.

In another sense, too, that distance had never been wider.

"Sucker!" was the last word from Harrelson in the Colorado kill zone.

There was a difference, sure. Bolan accepted the sucker tag, and wore it with weary pride.

Where would the world be, he wondered, when all the "suckers" were gone.

EPILOG

Time was back inside the frames, where it belonged, and Mack Bolan was enjoying the view.

The air was crisp and clean, thin but free, and the ski slopes were neatly packed with a fine dry bed of fresh happiness.

The president was smiling as he slipped past the viewpoint and glided on down the run, flanked by a gallery of admiring onlookers and the ever-present platoons of nervous treasury men.

Bolan smiled wearily and stepped into the telephone booth. Red Base and White Base might never have existed, for all the evidence they'd left behind. They had vanished, as had the forces that occupied them—and the will o' the wisp captain of infantry who'd commanded them.

Some things never vanished, though, thank God. Leo Turrin's droll voice crowded the connection with a perky, "Juno Two, is this who I hope it is?"

"The president is enjoying the slope," Bolan reported. "How are things in crazyland?"

"Still crazy," Turrin said, chuckling. "Hal is out beating some stars off of a couple of redfaced generals, but I guess things are pretty well intact. For the moment. By the way—he, uh, killed that regional alert on that Bolan guy. Seems that someone saw the guy down in Mexico or somewhere exotic like that. How, uh, how's the military picture in Colorado this morning?"

"Bright and clear," Bolan said. "I've just been hanging around, looking for a cornpone colonel, but I guess the guy is no diehard. He very gracefully withdrew."

"He'll be bouncing back again someday," Turrin said.

"I'm sure he will. We'll have to watch for that, won't we."

The little guy chuckled. "With bated breath. I, uh, I get a note of disappointment from Manhattan but no death wishes. I guess that marriage is still healthy enough. So watch yourself. They'll be trying again."

Bolan said, "Yeah, I'll be watching the movements. You too, Sticker. Keep the nose twitching."

"Oh, sure. Lot of good it did this time."

"It saved a president."

"The hell it did! We all know what saved the president today, Striker—and so does he."

"Hell of a note," Bolan said sourly. "You should have seen the guy, out there trying to look natural and happy in a wedge of bodyguards. There should be a better way."

"You think of it, he'll buy it," Turrin said. "After today, the congress may insist on portable bunkers for the guy."

"Speaking of buying," Bolan said.

"Yeah?"

"There's a nice lady up here who lost her all in the cause of the night. Tell Hal. The U.S. Government owes the lady a ski resort—and not a second class one, either. I expect to see Snow Trails Lodge rising again, and every bit as good as anything in Vail or Aspen."

"Okay. I'll put in your order. Anything else?"

"Peace," Bolan said.

"Oh yeah, sure."

Bolan chuckled and hung up. He returned to the warwagon and headed her north.

Snow Trails lay north.

Also a nice lady and a gutsy kid who maybe wouldn't mind a third hand around for a few days. There was some rebuilding to be done, some trails to ski, and perhaps even a dream or two to be rebuilt.

Peace, yeah—maybe. For a few days.

Then back to the kill zones . . . wherever they may be found.